SPECIAL MESSAGE TO READERS

This book is published under the auspices of

THE ULVERSCROFT FOUNDATION

(registered charity No. 264873 UK)

Established in 1972 to provide funds for research, diagnosis and treatment of eye diseases. Examples of contributions made are: —

A new Children's Assessment Unit at Moorfield's Hospital, London.

•

Twin operating theatres at the Western Ophthalmic Hospital, London.

•

A Chair of Ophthalmology at the University of Leicester.

•

The establishment of a Royal Australian College of Ophthalmologists "Fellowship".

You can help further the work of the Foundation by making a donation or leaving a legacy. Every contribution, no matter how small, is received with gratitude. Please write for details to:

THE ULVERSCROFT FOUNDATION,
The Green, Bradgate Road, Anstey,
Leicester LE7 7FU, England.
Telephone: (0116) 236 4325

In Australia write to:
THE ULVERSCROFT FOUNDATION,
c/o The Royal Australian College of Ophthalmologists,
27, Commonwealth Street, Sydney,
N.S.W. 2010.

Love is
a time of enchantment:
in it all days are fair and all fields
green. Youth is blest by it,
old age made benign:
the eyes of love see
roses blooming in December,
and sunshine through rain. Verily
is the time of true-love
a time of enchantment — and
Oh! how eager is woman
to be bewitched!

BEAU BARRON'S LADY

The love affair between Bess, a young ignorant girl from the slums, and Beau Barron, the high-born rake who moves in Court circles, seems doomed. Their ways part, but Bess is passionately determined on revenge when their child is born dead. Married to a humble pot-man, it seems she will never achieve her ambition — but fate plays odd tricks. The widowed Bess marries an earl and enters Barron's world, where her stormy love-hate battle with him begins.

Books by Pamela Bennetts
in the Ulverscroft Large Print Series:

MIDSUMMER-MORNING
THE LOVING HIGHWAYMAN
RUBY
LADY OF THE MASQUE

PAMELA BENNETTS

BEAU BARRON'S LADY

Complete and Unabridged

ULVERSCROFT
Leicester

First published in Great Britain in 1981 by
Robert Hale Limited
London

First Large Print Edition
published November 1994
by arrangement with
Robert Hale Limited
London

British Library CIP Data

Bennetts, Pamela
Beau Barron's lady.—Large print ed.—
Ulverscroft large print series: romance
I. Title
823.914 [F]

ISBN 0-7089-3181-2

Published by
F. A. Thorpe (Publishing) Ltd.
Anstey, Leicestershire

Set by Words & Graphics Ltd.
Anstey, Leicestershire
Printed and bound in Great Britain by
T. J. Press (Padstow) Ltd., Padstow, Cornwall

This book is printed on acid-free paper

Acknowledgements

I am much indebted to the authors of the following works, for without their help I could not have written this book:

The Life and Times of Beau Brummell: Carlo Maria Franzero

Leisure & Pleasure in the 19thC.: Stella Margetson

The Life & Times of George IV: Alan Palmer

The Georgian Gentleman: Michael Brander

The Bucks and Bawds of London Town: Kinsman de Barri

A History of Everyday Things in England: 1733 – 1851: Marjorie and C. H. B. Quennell

The Age of Illusion: James Laver

The Regency (Costume): Marion Sichel

Handbook of English Costume 19C.: C. Willett Cunnington and

Phillis Cunnington
A Dictionary of Historical Slang:
Eric Partridge — abridged by
Jacqueline Simpson
Carriages: Jacques Damase
The Coaching Age:
David Mountfield
Royal Courts of Fashion:
Norman Hartnell
Costume and Fashion 1760 – 1920:
Jack Cassin-Scott
The English Abigail:
Dorothy Margaret Stuart

1

"HURRY! My dear Charles, are you mad?"

For a moment, George Brummell's slender fingers were stilled on the delicate starched cravat, eyebrows raised a mere fraction. It was the nearest thing to emotion which he permitted himself in public. Emotions were not *bon ton*; he himself had decreed it so.

"I am creating a miracle. How can I hurry?"

Sir Charles Barron sighed and slumped lower in his chair. George might lead the fashionable world with his unique style and personal fastidiousness, but it took him, and his unfortunate valet, Robinson, hours every morning to achieve the perfection of the dark morning-coat without a wrinkle to mar its magnificence, and skin-tight buckskin breeches, which had to be eased on inch by inch. Two men attended to his coiffeur, two more to his gloves, one responsible for cutting the fingers, the other for the thumbs.

"It looks all right to me," said Charles finally, and without much hope. "Very well, in fact."

Brummell removed the stock, unhurriedly and handed it to Robinson, hovering anxiously at his master's elbow.

"Take this away; it offends me. Be kind enough to hand me a fresh one, and inform Sir Charles that I was unaware that his opinion on such matters had become so important."

Barron gave a slight laugh.

"Give him another, there's a good fellow. We've got to get to White's before nightfall. And tell your master not to waste time trying to put me down. I'm impervious to snubs, even his."

Brummell's rather small, pouting mouth moved slightly as he turned to regard Barron's long, lean figure. He had to admit that the dun-coloured coat was really rather good, and those strong, sinewy legs made the light pantaloons and shining Hessians things worthy of admiration. The almost colourless eyes moved upwards. Yes, Lady Jersey was right: Charles was most damnably handsome. Lips too thin, perhaps, and eyes far too sardonic, but the Beau had no quarrel with that. The chin and jaw were strong, the nose positively arrogant, but the bones of his cheeks would have put Adonis to shame.

"I suppose you threw your clothes on in about an hour." Brummell turned back to the mirror. "That stock is quite disgraceful."

"There's nothing wrong with it, and if you must know it took me only half an hour. Hadn't got the time to waste. I've ridden up from Brighton, breakfasted with Alvanley, bought a pair of greys, and paid my respects to Lady Cowper."

"Good God, Charles, I was right. You are mad."

A final flick of the crisp muslin, the important task of donning the gloves, and the Beau was finally ready.

"No target practice this morning?"

"That too, of course." Barron rose from the chair to tower some six inches over Brummell. "I think Pengelly is at last getting used to it."

"If I were your valet, and if you insisted on shooting small objects from off the top of my head, I should never reconcile myself to your eccentricities. I'd rather go and live in the workhouse."

"I doubt that." Charles was dry. "Somehow I do not see the workhouse as your true *milieu*."

"Perhaps not. Robinson, the silver and jade snuff-box to-day, I think."

Robinson's nimble fingers moved unerringly over the vast collection set out on a mahogany table beneath the window. When Brummell had first started to acquire the exquisite trifles, his valet had regarded them as one more dratted thing to be attended to, unable to distinguish one from another. Now, he was as proud of them as the Beau himself, expert in selecting the one his master wanted.

He grunted with relief as the door closed behind the Beau and his friend. He was proud of Brummell, of course; who wouldn't be? But five hours to prepare him for his afternoon appearance would be followed by an equally long period to re-dress him for the evening.

Whilst Robinson began to collect the discarded stocks, Brummell and Charles strolled slowly towards White's. Barron acknowledged a few of his friends with a brief lifting of the tall beaver hat, but Brummell's gaze was fixed firmly on the middle distance. Very few had the honour of a recognition from him, and it was not until a carriage pulled up close beside them that he was forced to stop.

A *grande dame*, clad in a dazzling array of jewellery and a flimsy gown fit for a girl half her age, stood four-square in Brummell's path, her air coy, her expression determined. The world was watching, and she had no intention of letting the odious Mr Brummell pass her by yet again.

"Mr Brummell, I declare."

"Yes, your grace." George's voice was toneless. "Or so I'm led to believe."

Her laugh was forced. The man was impossible; a jumped-up grandson of a valet, who'd had the good fortune to catch the Prince of Wales's eye some years before, and had landed himself a cornetcy in the prince's own regiment, the 10th Hussars. And how typical that the Beau had left the Hussars abruptly when they had been posted to Manchester, declaring that he had not signed on for foreign service.

"His Highness is giving a ball at Carlton House." The smile remained fixed, and she took a step or two sideways to make sure that Brummell couldn't slip past her. "Will you be there?"

Up went the eyebrows, and the duchess could feel blood seeping unbecomingly into her plump cheeks.

"Of course. The prince wishes the ball to be a success, doesn't he? How could it be so, if I were not there?"

Her grace's mouth opened, but the Beau had raised his hat and contrived to pass on, leaving her totally outraged.

"Really, George." Barron gave a reluctant laugh. "Isn't a duchess good enough for you nowadays?"

"She married a duke; that is quite a different matter. Ah, here we are at last. Thank God there will be no raddled hags inside to disturb me."

The two men took their seats in the bow window, a spot jealously reserved for a chosen few. The lords Worcester, Alvanley, Foley and Sefton; the Duke of Argyll, the dandy, 'Poodle' Byng, Sir Lumley Skeffington and 'Ball' Hughes, together with Brummell, and Sir Charles, the latter acknowledged the most noted whip of the day, and much admired for his 'bottom', or fortitude, and his bizarre behaviour, which never ceased to fascinate his contemporaries.

Charles was an incurable gambler, his luck veering from winning sixty thousand pounds one night to losing a like sum the next. Since the whole of polite society gambled as readily as it breathed, the high stakes put up by Barron made him an object of veneration to his fellows, whilst half the women in London were in love with him. He was handsome, dangerous, oblivious to caution. He treated the fair sex with rather less care than he did his bloodstock, and they adored him for it.

Brummell took his place, aware that every eye was upon him, noting the new way in which his cravat was tied, jealous of the lyrical smoothness of the cut-away coat; green with envy at the shine of his Hessians, which Robinson rubbed for hours on end with the froth of vintage champagne.

"Hear you made good time from Brighton, Charles." Argyll shifted in his chair. "Damned if I know how you do it, but you'll end by breaking your neck. Mark my words."

"Oh, I do." Barron raised his quizzing-glass and studied the duke. "How much did you bet on me."

"Two thousand."

"Then you've made a good profit. And you, Alvanley?"

"Only five hundred."

"Really, how short-sighted of you, m'dear fellow. Not losing your nerve, I hope."

"What about your nerve, sir?" Foley sniggered. "Didn't you lose a packet last night at the tables? Ten thousand, wasn't it?"

"I've no idea." Charles dropped the glass and let his frosty hazel eyes travel slowly over the unfortunate Foley. "One doesn't count one's losses, does one, or gains either, for that matter."

The Beau's lips twitched.

"Well said," he murmured under his breath. "I really do think my influence is making itself felt at last."

"I lost too." 'Poodle' Byng was gloomy. "Got a mountain of bills to meet. Blasted tradesmen are forever at me to pay them."

"Burn 'em," advised Barron. "I never pay bills. Infernal shop-keepers get above themselves if you do."

The talk became general, every man and woman of note being carefully dissected by the leaders of White's, who blackballed upstarts with ruthless unconcern, and whose opinion could make or break a soireé, a ball, or a reputation with equal ease.

Later that day, the idle chatter gave way to serious business, and the men in White's held their breath as they watched Barron playing macao for stakes which made even the most hardened blink.

The game went one way, then the other, drink flowing until some members sagged into a stupor in their chairs. Charles drank too, but his eyes under their slumberous lids were as alert as ever, his thin, strong hands as steady as a rock.

When the climax came, it was as if every man sighed simultaneously, a hushed ripple of sound running round the table as the final card was flipped over.

"It seems this is my lucky night," said Charles finally. "Sorry, my dear fellow."

Sir John Masterton was grim as he looked up at Beau Barron. The man was as cool as a cucumber, almost disinterested in the fifty thousand pounds which he had just won. Masterton felt sick, and there was a line of perspiration along his brow. He knew he dared not shew his fear, or he'd be finished. Everyone was watching him, and he had to brace himself if he were not to be ruined socially. Ruined! He bit back an exclamation. That was precisely what he was: ruined. The horses would have to go; the mansion in Surrey too. What his mother would say he dared not dwell upon, and now her insistence that he should marry the frumpish heiress from Northumberland would have to be accepted.

"No matter." He got the words out at last, proud that his voice was without a tremor. "There's always to-morrow."

"Just what I say." Barron rose to his

feet, finishing his glass of brandy in one gulp. "Always another day."

"Not for him," said Worcester, when Sir John had moved off. "Poor devil, he's done for."

"Shouldn't play if he can't afford to lose."

"You can't always afford to lose, Charles, but that hasn't stopped you, eh?"

"Ah, my dear Worcester, but I bear a charmed life, don't you know. Well, I'm off."

"Never going to drive in that state, surely?"

Charles's quizzing-glass turned on Skeffington, his mouth a straight line. "Suggestin' I'm in my cups, Lumley?"

Skeffington moved uncomfortably. Barron had a way of looking at a man which made him feel one inch high.

"No, no, but . . . "

"Of course I'm driving: now, and first thing tomorrow morning too. The beasts need the exercise, and so do I. Brummell, your servant: my lords."

"Kill himself one day: I'm always saying so."

"So you are, Argyll, and very tedious it's becoming." George Brummell was tart. "Leave Charles to go to perdition in his own way. Won't do you any good to fall out with him. Something about Barron . . . "

"Never tell me he disturbs you, George." Alvanley poured himself more claret. "Can't believe anyone could do that."

"Quite right, no one does, but Charles is . . . well . . . never mind. It's time I went home. Your arm, Skeffington."

As the Beau and Sir Lumley left St James's Street, Charles Barron was driving his high perch-phaeton through the dark streets of London at a very fast, but finely controlled, speed. The horses' eyes rolled wildly when the whip touched their flanks, their nostrils flaring as hooves clattered madly over the cobbles.

Charles had no idea where he was, and cared even less. The club had been hot, and he welcomed the sharper night air. He was vaguely aware that the West End of London was well behind him, and that the houses and shops on each side were mean and shabby as he crossed the river to the south bank.

He was contemplating turning back, when suddenly someone was in the road in front of him. The moon shewed an outline: almost too late to bring the panting horses to an abrupt halt. His voice was curt as he gripped the reins and shouted to the bays. Then he flung himself off the driving-seat, dropping lightly to the ground, furious with whoever had got in his way. He cared not a jot for any surprise or alarm which they might have felt; his thoughts were only for the horses which had cost a small fortune.

"God Almighty! What in the name of Hades d'you think you're doing?"

One strong hand gripped the figure lying in the road, hauling it up with a roughness which made it screech.

"Hell's teeth!" Barron swore aloud. "A wench, eh? What's the matter with you, you silly trollop? Are you trying to kill yourself?"

If Charles expected a contrite apology, he was disappointed. The girl, no more than seventeen, wrenched herself away and spat at him with all the fire of a vixen defending her young.

"Pig! Think yer own the road, do yer? Must be boneheaded, ridin' like that. Might 'ave run right over me, you so . . ."

Barron's initial consternation was over, and he closed iron fingers round her wrist.

"Don't talk to me like that, you slut, or I'll lay my whip across your backside. What are you doing out at this time of night?"

"Mind yer own bloody business, and if you lays an 'and on me, I'll scream blue murder."

"If I don't strangle you first," he returned silkily. "Now hold still, and let me look at you."

The girl jerked in his hold, but this time she was powerless to free herself as Barron pulled the shawl back from her head and began to look her over as if she were a mare he was proposing to purchase.

Her hair was a tumble of red-gold; not clean, but still breathtaking. Her skin was designed by Nature to be milk-white, but now it was grimed with dirt. He considered the large green eyes and small delicate nose with some surprise, his lids dropping to conceal the admiration which her lovely mouth aroused in him. Black as a chimney-sweep's apprentice, but a beauty for all that.

The appraisal moved down to her body. A ragged dress, scarcely covering the full, thrusting breasts, straining over hips which roused an unexpected lust in him.

"What's your name, girl?" he asked finally. "Do you live near here?"

"What's that to you?"

"Answer me civilly, or I'll teach you some manners in a way you won't like. Your name?"

She was sulky.

"Bess."

"Bess what?"

"Hathaway, and let go o' me wrist. You're 'urtin' me."

"I intended to, and I'll hurt you a good deal more if you don't watch your tongue. Why aren't you at home? Looking for a drunk to rob, are you?"

Bess glared at him. She had been

thoroughly shaken by the sight of the rearing mounts coming at her, certain that her days were numbered. And, as if that weren't enough, here was this fop, with his expensive evening-coat, knee-breeches, silk stockings and buckled shoes, nearly breaking her arm, and threatening her with worse.

Then she took a closer look at his face. She couldn't see much, because the moon was half hidden by a cloud, but it was sufficient. She could feel her blood tingle: a new and disturbing sensation made her shiver. She wanted to strike back at him, but she couldn't.

"Well, I'm waiting." Charles was short. "Why aren't you home in bed?"

"I run away, that's why. Me pa beat me, and I run. 'Spect I'll go back in the mornin'."

"I'm not surprised that your father beat you. So would I, if I were in the unfortunate position of having you for a daughter."

The red lips pouted, eyes flickering with renewed temper, but much to Bess's chagrin words would not come.

"Well, Bess Hathaway, what are we

going to do with you? Can't spend the night in the street, can you?"

"Why not?" She found her voice at last. "Done it enough times before."

"Have you indeed? Are you a virgin?"

Bess blushed unexpectedly.

It was not an age for the mealy-mouthed. Men and women spoke bluntly and without reserve on the most intimate of subjects, yet that particular question coming from this man drove Bess back into silence.

"I see. You're not."

She took a deep breath, and Barron watched with interest the exciting rise of her half-concealed bosom.

"As a matter of fact I am. So there!"

"You surprise me." He let her go, and raised the quizzing-glass. "Can't see a lot of you, of course, but it'll do. I would have thought you'd have known many men by now."

"Well, I don't, and I'm goin' now." She started to back away. "Didn't mean to get in the way of the 'orses."

Before she could turn and run, Charles had caught her by the shoulders.

"Oh no, my pretty Bess, you don't get

off that easily. There's a price to pay for what you've done."

Her mouth dried, fear making her cringe.

"Don't beat me." Her mouth was unsteady. "I'm sore enough, for me pa's got an 'eavy 'and."

"I wasn't going to beat you, my foolish brat. Rather the opposite, in fact. Come, get up on the seat with me."

"What! Go with you? Where?"

"To a house I know."

"But where?"

She found herself hoisted into the driver's seat as if she were made of air. Since she knew her curves were rather too ample, despite lack of food, she marvelled at the strength of this strange, unpredictable man, who was now beside her, urging the horses on as he turned the phaeton round.

"Near Covent Garden."

"What we goin' there for?"

"Oh come!" He shot her a cynical glance. "You're not that stupid, surely?"

One part of her wanted to jump from the carriage, regardless of the speed they were picking up: another part kept her still, the closeness of the man, smelling of some light, costly cologne, making her heart thud uneasily.

It seemed no time at all before they had reached their destination. So much was happening so quickly that Bess hardly realised what was going on. The house in a side-street was just a vague impression. She knew her captor was being welcomed with fawning enthusiasm, and that gold coins were passing from one hand to another.

Then she found herself in a bedroom, with the man locking the door behind them. She had no illusions, and, strangely, no desire to fight, but she put up a token resistance.

"I'm hungry."

"Good, all the better, but if you eat now you'll go to sleep, and that's not what I had in mind. I'll feed you later, although by the look of you you're not starving."

"'Aven't 'ad a morsel since yesterday mornin'."

Barron was removing his coat, pausing to look at her carefully.

"Is that the truth?"

"I've said, 'aven't I?"

"Women are born liars."

"Well, I'm not, leastways, not about that. 'Ad a crust of bread. We're poor, you see."

"Mm." He nodded. "I believe you. You can eat until you make yourself sick when I've done with you. Get undressed."

"Don't want to."

"I don't give a damn whether you do or not. Get rid of that rag, or I'll tear it off myself."

She swallowed hard, but there was no escaping what was about to happen, nor did she really want to get away. In the light of the candles the man was stunningly good to look at, and rich too, judging by his apparel.

"What a voluptuous little creature you are," said Barron, "although perhaps little is the wrong word to use. Yes, by God, you are a goodly armful, aren't you?"

Beau Barron was as expert at making love as he was at racing, gambling, and firing his well-balanced pistols. Whether the woman in question was a duchess or a drab, he treated her with the same gentleness and courtesy in bed. But when the preliminaries were over, so was the gentleness, and Bess gasped aloud as his fierce passion opened the floodgates of her own untapped emotions.

She was not naturally shy or retiring, and the fact that she had escaped the attentions of other men had been a matter of sheer good luck. But as Charles made love to her, she responded with an enthusiastic vigour which made her body burn like fire and her head spin.

She wanted it to go on forever, this ecstasy which made every part of her feel vividly alive, but of course it didn't, and she felt a curious mixture of supreme happiness and emptiness when Barron dressed swiftly and ordered the food he had promised.

She began to eat ravenously, glancing shyly at Charles. He looked so different now: every strand of his dark hair in place, each fold of his cravat in perfect order. The savage predator was gone; only the elegant Corinthian remained. She wondered for a second whether she had imagined what she had shared with him on the bed in the corner, but it hadn't been a dream. It had been very real, turning her from a girl into a woman in the space of fifteen minutes.

"Most enjoyable," he said, and smiled slightly. "And most surprising. Here's a sixpence for you."

"Thanks." She pocketed it, quite unoffended. It would be useful to her mother, who had many hungry mouths to feed. "'Ow am I goin' ter get 'ome?"

"I've no idea." He picked up his whip and gloves, making for the door. "When you've stuffed yourself to bursting point, no doubt some solution will come to you. I'll see you here in one week's time, at midnight. Be punctual. I don't like to be kept waiting."

She stared at the closed door, the problem of how to get back to Southwark completely forgotten. He wanted to see her again: wanted to make love to her. She was filled with excitement as she began to bundle the rest of the food into the cloth, for it was far too good to leave behind.

He wanted her, and a week wasn't very long to wait.

* * *

Nearly three months later, Bess sat on the side of the bed in the house in Covent Garden. She'd come to know the bedroom very well; to her, it was as near to heaven as she ever hoped to get.

She'd made friends with the madam who ran the house, a big, burly woman, who needed no bully boys to rid herself of trouble-makers. Mrs Rook had taken to Bess, because she said, Bess reminded her of one of her sisters who had died young.

From Mrs Rook, Bess learned a lot about Beau Barron, for the brothel-keeper prided herself on knowing all about the *beau monde* as well as her own seedy world. Young bucks often came to the stews, slumming, and after too much wine they tended to talk. Charles was a friend of the Prince of Wales, and of Mr Brummell, of whom Mrs Rook spoke with awe.

Bess listened avidly to all the tales: she wanted to know everything about Barron and his friends. She gaped at the stories of his suicidal racing, of his reckless gambling, and the mad escapades in which he indulged, which made him such a favourite of a blasé society.

When he came in, she rose at once, bobbing respectfully, for Charles, true to his word, had taught her a few manners since they had first met.

"Well?" He removed his coat, and gave an approving nod. "You look better for a new gown. It suits you."

She flushed with pleasure.

"It was ever so good of you to send it. I'm reel grateful."

"So you should be, you hussy. It's far too expensive for you."

She chuckled, for the amusement in his eyes told her he was teasing her. She wanted to reach up and kiss the corner of his mouth, but she knew better. It was not for her to say when their love-making would begin.

Barron studied the exquisite colour of Bess's cheeks and the inviting warmth of her mouth. He thought himself a trifle demented to come here every week, simply to meet a girl like Bess, but there was something about her which stopped him from breaking off the liaison.

It was not just the richness of her body, which she gave so willingly, and which aroused in him a sensation he had never felt before. She had a quality in her he hadn't found in any other woman; a kind of gallantry, not bending to her poverty, her sadistic father, or hunger and dirt. She had the spirit to rise above such things, and rise with a smile and a laugh which weren't forced. That was true bottom, and he respected her for it.

"I've somethin' to tell yer," she said, as Barron began to take off his waistcoat. "Don't know what you'll say, but you've got ter know."

"Oh, what's that?"

He went on with what he was doing, and she hesitated until he repeated the question rather more sharply.

"I'm with child." She said it quietly, holding herself in, waiting for his reaction. "No doubt about it. Old Mother Moss said so, and she's never wrong."

Slowly Charles turned to look at her, his frown giving her the first warning.

"Oh?"

"Aye, but it won't make no difference to us, will it?" She was pleading with him, but almost instantly she knew that she had lost. "It won't, will it?"

"Difference? Of course it will; don't be ridiculous. What do you imagine I could do with an illegitimate child?"

"It wouldn't be no bother to you. I'd care for it, just so long as I could see you each week, like now."

"No." He was curt, reaching for his coat again. "No, it's out of the question. What's done is done."

She could feel the tears beginning to roll down her cheeks, her stomach hollow.

"You won't let me come 'ere again?"

"Come as often as you like, but you won't find me here."

"Oh Gawd." She buried her face in her hands. "What am I goin' ter do?"

"Go home, where you belong."

"Me father'll kill me when 'e 'ears what's 'appened."

"Of course he won't. He's probably fathered a dozen bastards himself. Go home."

He reached into his pocket and laid a

pile of coins on the table.

"Take this. That'll keep you and the child until you can go whoring again."

He was deliberately cruel: he had to be, to withstand the look in Bess's eyes. It had to be done. A complete cut, severing their intimacy once and for all, but he didn't want to watch what he was doing to her.

"Whoring? Is that 'ow you think of me?"

His laugh was derisive.

"Why not? How do you think of yourself, pray?"

Bess sat down, her tears done. Inside, she felt as if she were turning to stone. She hadn't expected Barron to acknowledge the baby openly, but it had never occurred to her that he would wipe her out of his life as if she had never existed.

She had loved him so much, and had allowed herself to believe that he had had some feeling for her. His kisses and the touch of his hand had fooled her completely, but now she was staring at the stark truth. She meant nothing to him, and never had.

She straightened up, her native courage reasserting itself, born of fury.

"I'll never forgive you for that," she said in a small, tight voice. "Not for as long as I live. I'll make yer pay for those words, Charles Barron, just see if I don't. One day you'll grovel for callin' me names like that."

"I've said nothing which isn't true." The tall beaver was tilted at just the right angle over his dark curls, cut *à la Brutus*, his gloved hand on his cane. "You are a bawd, and a careless one. You made your bed; now lie on it."

* * *

Outside, Charles paused. Bess's announcement had shaken him, although he should have realised what could happen as a result of their relationship. He knew he'd hurt her deeply, and that he'd been unjust. It wasn't her fault: at least, it was no more her doing than his. For one insane second he considered going back; taking her in his arms, and telling her not to worry. Then his eyes grew cold, and he began to descend the stairs. It was a ludicrous notion, and not one to be entertained. He had his life to lead, and Bess could play no part in it, particularly with an unwanted infant in tow. He'd enjoyed her, but now it was done.

He was getting into his curricle when he stopped yet again. He wouldn't see Bess any more. Her gaiety and courage and her sweetly plump body were things of the past. He wouldn't hear her infectious laugh, or feel the hunger in her for his loving. Then he shrugged. It couldn't be helped, and there were a hundred girls like her to be had.

It had been a pleasant interlude, but now it was over. As far as he was concerned, Bess Hathaway was dead.

* * *

Bess left ten minutes after Barron. She had his money, but not him. She wouldn't let herself consider the fact that she would never see him again. Anger and thoughts of retribution were easier to handle as she made her way to *The Pig and Whistle*, a tavern where she went every week to wait until it was time to join Charles.

For the first time in her life she had real money, and she intended to use some of it to get blind drunk, so that she need not think, or feel, or hurt for at least an hour or two.

Fred Walton, the pot-man, served her, as he always did. Fred treated her like a lady, wiping the rough wooden table with his cloth before setting down the glass of gin.

She nodded to him, hardly seeing the tall, gangling figure, thinning hair, and large brown eyes. She liked Fred, for he was gentle and kind, and if his big hands and feet made him appear clumsy it was more than compensated for by the quiet comfort he exuded.

Walton watched with concern as she ordered glass after glass, biting his lip as laughter turned to tears, and tears to near unconsciousness. When she slipped from the bench and fell heavily to the floor, he ignored the raucous laughter of the men nearby, and took off his apron, making his excuses to the landlord, Bill Sugarwhite.

He never knew how he managed to get the groaning girl up to his single room in a nearby lodging-house, which he shared with mice and cockroaches, but somehow he did it. He wished he had a proper blanket to wrap her in, sacrificing his threadbare coat to tuck round her, for July or no, it was chilly.

For the rest of the night he sat by her side on a rickety chair, watching her toss and turn, seeing the moisture run from beneath her lashes. When the first pale light crept through the tiny window, he went downstairs to beg some hot water from the landlady, Mrs Timothy. Many would have been piqued by so early a disturbance, but Jess Timothy was fond of Fred, and was always up and about by five o'clock.

When he explained his predicament, he was given not only hot water, but a pot with precious brown leaves in it, and a cup with a handle. He hurried upstairs with his treasures to find Bess stirring.

"Oh Jesus, me 'ead!" She sat up with difficulty, not sure at first where she was, nor what had happened. "Gawd! Where am I?"

Then she saw Walton, and the events of the previous night came flooding back.

The torment was almost unbearable, but she wouldn't let Fred see it. Pain was a private thing to be kept to oneself.

"'Allo, Fred. 'Ow did I get 'ere? Don't remember comin'."

He grinned.

"You didn't, leastways, not by yourself. 'Ad to 'alf carry you most of the way. 'Ere, drink this. Make you feel better."

"Thanks." She sipped the tea gratefully. It was hot and strong, and took some of the misery away. "That's a fair treat. So you 'ad to lug me up 'ere, did you? No feather, am I?"

She sobered as he sat down beside her again.

"Suppose you know what's 'appened. Everyone knows everyone else's business around 'ere.

"I'd 'eard summat."

"Reckon you 'eard the lot." She was bleak. "Made a fool of meself, I did. Let that dandified swine take me, 'cos I thought 'e was fond of me. Christ, what a stupid bitch I am. Soon as I told 'im about the kid, 'e was off. Gave me money, and told me to go whoring again."

She turned her head.

"Knew about the young 'un on the way, did yer?"

He nodded, and she gave a short laugh.

"Thought so: 'spect they all do by now. Well, that's it. Shan't see 'is 'igh and mightiness again, or so 'e thinks, but one day I'll pay 'im out for what 'e's done. 'E won't do this to me, and not regret it. I'll make 'im suffer like what 'e's makin' me suffer, just see if I don't."

Fred watched Bess's distorted face. She looked like a different girl, and it disturbed him.

"Don't say things like that. Not good for the baby."

"Fat lot you know about it."

She was pettish, but gradually the terrible anger was beginning to retreat.

"Well, maybe not." Walton was looking down at his big, bony hands. "But I knows one thing."

"What's that?"

"The bairn should 'ave a father. Every kid's got a right to that."

"A father! 'E won't be no father to my child."

"No, but I will, if you'll let me."

Bess sank back against the thin pillow and gaped at him. "You! Fred, what you sayin'?"

"That I wants to marry you, if you'll 'ave me."

"But that's nonsense!" She was studying his face, seeing him in a new light. "Why'd yer want to marry a bulker like me, 'specially now?"

"'Cos I love you," he replied simply, and gave her a shy smile. "Don't say it: I knows you don't love me, but that don't matter. I'll be good to you, and faithful."

"'Spect you will," she said dryly, some of her astonishment fading. "But 'ow do you know I'll be the same?"

"I don't. It's a chance I'll 'ave to take."

"You're balmy, Fred Walton, d'yer know that?" She didn't know what to say, stunned by such self-sacrifice. "What's in it for you?"

"I'll 'ave you as me wife, and right proud I'll be of it."

"Well . . . " She hesitated. It was a way out, yet she liked Fred, reluctant to make use of him. "I suppose . . . "

"Then say yes. Oh, Bess, do say yes!"

She smiled, her hand over his.

"I'll work my fingers to the bone for you, I swear it."

"No need for that," he returned sharply. "Don't want my wife sweating for her keep. I've got a steady job."

"And poorly paid." She grimaced. "All right for one mouth; three's different. No, I'll work, never fear."

"We'll see. Well, will you?"

Their eyes met. He could see the wounds in her, knowing she was bleeding for a man who had hurt her almost beyond curing. He had heard all about Barron, and had no delusions. Bess had worshipped Sir Charles; she still did, in spite of what had happened. Bess saw the plea and the need in Fred, and wanted to cry, but she knew that once she let the tears come they would never stop.

"Yes, Fred, I will, and I'm right grateful."

"Don't want gratitude."

"Can't give you anything else."

"I've already said it don't matter."

She sighed deeply.

"No, perhaps it's better without that kind of love. That sort can kill you inside. 'Ere, give us a kiss and seal the bargain."

He hesitated, and now her laughter was warm again as she pulled him close to her.

"Old silly. Not afraid of me, are you? Better not be, since we're goin' to share a bed. Come on, kiss me."

Fred went out into the fresh July morning, walking on air. He could still feel Bess's moist lips on his own; smell her flesh as she had held him against her breast. He whistled gaily as he went off to the tavern, the happiest man in the world. Bess was going to be his wife.

Alone in the bedroom, Bess's gentleness was gone. She had kissed Fred, and, whilst doing so, had thought of Charles.

"I'll do for you, Charles Barron," she said aloud to the empty room. "If it takes me all me life, I'll do for yer."

Then she finished the last of the tea, turned over on her side, and fell asleep.

2

TWO weeks after the simple marriage ceremony Bess announced that she had purchased a brothel in Garnet Street, Covent Garden. At first, Fred was horrified. She was too young, he protested, and there was the baby on its way.

"All the more reason to make money," she said, and put her arms round him. "Now listen to me, Fred Walton. Maybe I'm young, but that's no bad thing. You know the stews round 'ere, same as I do, and they make a profit, the good ones, that is. Ours'll be reel good. Clean and neat, and no one need worry about wagging tongues."

"But . . . "

"It'll only be for a while, luv, just till we get on our feet. Then we'll stop. Maybe move to the country."

His face lightened.

"I'd like that. Brought up in the country, I was, and it'ud be good for the boy."

"Well, that's that then, but don't forget, it might be a girl."

"Bess." His alarm had returned. "Bess, you won't 'ave to . . . that is . . . it won't be you, 'oo 'as to . . . "

She threw back her head and laughed. It wasn't a pretty sound.

"Jesus, no, not me! Others can look after the customers; I'm just takin' the money."

Despite her youth, Bess was efficient. The streets round Covent Garden were vile in the extreme, and the house which she had bought lay between two notorious sluiceries, where hopeless men and women drowned their sorrows in jackey, and where the fouled pavements were tramped over by every down-at-heel trollop, pimp, pander, he-whore and pervert in the area.

There were brothels all round them, some good, some no more than cess-pools of vice. By Covent Garden itself, old Jewish women, raddled and filthy in their long black cloaks, gathered with their strings of young girls, selling them off for the night for the highest price they could get.

None of this deterred Bess. She hired cleaning women, and had her property scrubbed from attic to cellar. Cheap rugs were purchased, as well as bales of cotton for sheets and curtains. Each room had a chair, a table, a candlestick, and the all-important bed, with windows which Fred had cleaned until they sparkled.

Bess knew the neighbours resented her, and at first they threatened her for trying to snatch their trade away from them, but after a few sharp words, and even a blow or two from the buxom Bess, they slunk back into their hovels muttering, but no longer willing to take her on.

Her business was successful from the start. Her reputation for cleanliness and discretion grew, and gay young blades, seeking a night out, away from their own doorsteps, returned again and again, recommending Mrs Hathaway, as she called herself, to their friends.

When she had been there for two months, Bess decided that she needed some new dresses. Wasn't right for her, the proprietress of such a good place, to be seen in rags. Mrs Sugarwhite, at the tavern, told her of a woman living two streets away.

"Come down in the world, you might say," said the landlady regretfully. "Nice little body too; shame, I calls it. Sews a fair seam though, and doesn't overcharge. Why don't you see 'er? Name's Cotter."

Bess took her advice, and when she called upon Miss Cotter she found the seamstress had an attic room, where the light was good. Puffing upstairs, Bess cursed, wishing the baby would come soon, for she was growing too large for comfort, and for hard work.

Christine Cotter was a tiny mortal, with grey hair neatly curled, and a pretty dress of white muslin.

"Nice," said Bess, when she had been invited to sit down. "Looks good on you. Make it yerself?"

Christine blushed.

"Yes. I was given the material: a piece left over from an order. I am glad that you like it."

Bess was meditative. What Mrs Sugarwhite had said was true. Miss Cotter was a lady, with a soft voice and graceful movements. She looked about fifty, but perhaps bad luck and poverty had aged her prematurely. Her room was as clean as any of Bess's, but although scantily furnished, Bess's eagle eye noted that each piece was simple and restful to look at. There were no garish colours to jar; no fussy ornaments or gew-gaws.

Bess made a mental note, and turned back to Miss Cotter. She was interested in the seamstress, yet she didn't want to appear to pry. However, her first few tentative questions were readily answered, and, over a dish of tea, served in real china cups, she learned how Miss Cotter's father had gambled away his fortune and then taken his life; how her mother had died shortly afterwards of, so Christine said, a broken heart. With no relations willing to take her in, and no money, Miss Cotter had collected what remained of her parents' home, after the creditors had taken their pickings, and come to London to try to earn a living with the one skill she possessed: fine needlework and embroidery.

"I don't make a fortune," she said ruefully. "As you can see, much is wanting here, but I manage."

Bess didn't confess that Miss Cotter's room made her own establishment seem tawdry: instead, she studied Christine's thin frame and pinched face, and was blunt.

"Don't take enough victuals, Miss Cotter, that's your trouble."

She knew at once that she had offended, for the seamstress sat up like a ramrod, her eyes avoiding her visitor's.

"Don't mind me." Bess was embarrassed by her gaffe. "Don't know the right words to use to gentry, such as you."

"It is perfectly all right, Mrs Hathaway."

"But it isn't, and I'm reel sorry."

Bess knew better than to pursue the matter, but in no time at all she had managed to persuade Miss Cotter to work at the house in Garnet Street, and, naturally, when mid-day came all those on the premises were well-fed by Bess, who enjoyed making rich meat puddings and pies, and baking fruit tarts which were a delight to all who tasted them.

She watched Miss Cotter use her knife and fork with delicate precision, knowing how hungry she was. It was not only a lesson in table manners, but an insight into self-control, and one which Bess took to heart.

Soon after that, another unfortunate was taken under her wing. Roger Burnham lived next door. He had been a tutor, having received a first-class education, and spent three years at Cambridge. Drink had robbed him of his position with a rich man, and almost stolen his senses into the bargain. Now, however, money was harder to come by, and the sobering of Mr Burnham was not a pleasant thing to watch.

Fred gave him odd jobs about the house, which provided enough for a modest sup at the adjoining tavern, whilst Bess, worried by his cavernous cheeks and sunken eyes, fed him as one of her growing family.

It was as if she were the mother, and they her children, despite the fact that she was a mere eighteen, but in Bess's world women grew up quickly, and childhood was a very fleeting thing.

By one of life's crooked quirks, it was Burnham, humbly grateful to Bess, who broke the news to her which shattered the careful shell she had built around herself. Roger was always interested in news of that other world which he had left behind, and when the fops and bucks came down to the slums he contrived to sidle up to them and listen to the gossip of the day.

"Mr D'Arcy Matthers and Sir James Craig were in *The Pig and Whistle* last night. Very merry they were."

"Mm." Bess was listening with only half an ear, her mind on the need to change the sheets in the top two rooms before the evening trade began. "Know them, do you?"

"I did once." Burnham's mouth was drooping. "But they didn't recognise me, of course."

"Well, that's nice, and what did they have to say? And they probably didn't notice you, Mr Burnham, seein' they were chattin' so."

Bess was always quick to hear distress in others, urging him to forget the past and relate his tale. She wasn't interested herself, but Christine, who also clung tenaciously to the life she had once known, would want to hear what the latest talk was about.

"Sir Charles Barron is to marry. No one thought he would, for he likes his freedom, but it seems he's in such debt that there's no help for it but a rich wife."

"I remember my father talking of Sir Charles's father." Christine was animated, old things, long forgotten, making her eyes bright again. "Who is the bride-to-be?"

"The daughter of an Austrian count, and wealty as Croesus." Burnham shook his head. "Poor girl, she's very young, so Sir James said. She will have her hands full with a man like Beau Barron."

Fred was watching Bess anxiously, but his wife's face was like granite. What she was thinking or feeling he had no idea, but he knew he dared not ask.

Finally, Bess rose from the table, voice untroubled.

"If you've finished, Miss Cotter, perhaps you'd 'elp me with the beds, and then there's that hit 'o sarcenet I wants to talk ter you about."

"Of course, of course." Christine got up, flustered, in case Bess thought she was a gossip-monger. "I'm sorry if I . . . "

"Nothin' to be sorry about." Bess was as calm as a millpond. "Simply that there's a bit to do afore the evenin'"

But when the beds were done, and orders given for a dress to be made in the latest fashion of 1807, Miss Cotter slipped away, and Bess went to the window and stared out.

The hatred of Barron, which had sustained her since he had left, was melting before the agony which Burnham's words had roused. She could see Charles's face in her mind's eye, as if he were in the room with her, and could almost feel the cool, strong hands moving slowly and sensuously over her body.

"Oh Gawd," she whispered, and leaned her head against the curtain, letting the cheap cotton cover her face. "Oh Gawd, no! no!"

It was absurd of her to think that Barron wouldn't marry for one reason or another, yet now the news had been broken it was as if a scar inside her had opened up and was oozing blood.

"Charles, Charles! I could kill yer; straight I could."

She wished she could cry to get rid of the dam of sorrow building up, but she couldn't. Dry-eyed, she pulled herself together, patting the curtains into place. Too bright, they were. When she could afford it she'd get some like Miss Cotter's, which retained their elegance, faded though they were.

She forgot about curtains and good taste, her mind back on Charles. Whatever she said of him, and how often she said it, it made no difference. She wanted to destroy Barron; to make him suffer as she had suffered, but that didn't alter things.

She went downstairs to get on with her work, accepting the truth with a fortitude which Charles would have applauded.

She abhorred him, but she loved him with all her heart and she knew she'd go on doing so until the day she died.

* * *

For the next month Bess never stopped working. She drove herself as one possessed, ignoring Fred's urgent pleas to rest.

"If I rest, I think, and I don't want that," she told him. "Leave me be, luv, I'm all right."

But he knew she wasn't, and it broke his heart to watch her try to conceal her secret. He had always known, perhaps better than Bess herself, the depth of her love for Barron: he had accepted it philosophically, contenting himself with the warmth of her next to him at night, and her generous giving of herself to a man she didn't want.

Miss Cotter was worried too.

"It is not my business, Mr Walton," she said, watching the swollen body of Bess carrying heavy bundles of linen upstairs, "but there is a risk, you know. Can't you make her stop?"

He shook his head, and tried to smile.

"No, Miss, I wishes I could, for it tears me apart to see what she's doin' to 'erself, but . . . "

"She wasn't like this before." Miss Cotter gave a discreet cough. "It is nothing to do with me, I know, but I owe her so much, that if I could help it would give me much happiness. It was when Mr Burnham mentioned Sir

Charles's marriage, wasn't it? I saw her face."

Fred was surprised: he hadn't thought the seamstress would have known about loving of that kind.

"Aye, she knew 'im."

"Poor Mrs Walton." When there was no one about the name Hathaway was forgotten: that was just for the neighbours and the clients. "How I wish all men were as kind as you. Most of them cause such unhappiness, I've found."

Fred nodded, and they went their separate ways, but a few days later Bess stumbled downstairs, and couldn't get up. Christine was there, and saw at once what had happened. For once in her timid life she took charge, sending one of the scrubbing women for the midwife, and ordering Fred and Roger Burnham to lift the suffering Bess upstairs to her bed.

The midwife and her daughter came soon enough, but there wasn't much that they could do. Bess cried out until Fred put his hands over his ears to drown the noises which bit deep into him, and Miss Cotter, her task done, shrank back into her corner and wept for her friend.

When the baby came, premature and stillborn, the faces of the midwife and her daughter told Bess the truth before they opened their mouths.

"I'm glad," she shouted at them hysterically. "I'm glad it's dead, d'yer hear? Don't tell me what it was: I don't want to know. If I don't know, it'll be like it never existed."

The two women exchanged significant glances, and Bess yelled at them in helpless rage.

"No, you silly cows, I'm not off me 'ead. Don't you understand, you stupid ninnies? I've lost me child."

She turned her head away, her lips moving silently so that they couldn't hear the rest.

"I've lost Charles's child. Oh, sweet Jesus, I've lost it."

During the next two weeks, no one knew whether Bess would live or die. She had puerperal fever, and the doctor called in by Fred shook his head doubtfully.

"Can't tell, Mr Walton; no one could. Very sick woman, your wife, very sick. Just have to wait and see. Give her this draught when you can, and keep her warm. Nothing else to do."

Fred kept a vigil by her bed, wincing as he heard her call out for Charles in her delirium. He'd always told himself he was lucky to get what was left, but now, when Bess needed help, it wasn't her husband to whom she cried, but to a man who had probably forgotten her existence long since. Then Fred began to hate Barron as much as Bess did, although, of course, he admitted sadly to himself, she didn't really hate Sir Charles at all.

He wiped his nose on his sleeve, watching the fever devour his beloved Bess in its maw. She still loved Barron, and he, Fred, could do nothing about it. No matter how hard he tried, he couldn't have Bess's heart, because that belonged to the man who had brought her to a sick-bed, and to the point of death.

He buried his head in his hands and let his tears flow, for Bess was past noticing. As the doctor had said, he could only wait and see.

* * *

Almack's on the night of December the 9th was *en feŝe*. No one was quite sure what the celebration was about, and nobody cared particularly.

The fearsome, high-born ladies who ruled the club with a rod of iron were watching the dancers with disinterested eyes; they were too busy dissecting Beau Barron's wife to worry about the music, the glittering jewels and fabulous gowns, or the graceful steps of those on the floor.

Lady Jersey, who prided herself on her rudeness and glacial stare, wore high-waisted, low-cut white muslin, with jewelled combs in her hair, and a painted fan in her hand which twitched impatiently to and fro.

"The girl's nothing but a frump," she said shortly. "Why, I swear her complexion is as dark as any gypsy's."

Lady Sefton, a kinder and more amiable woman, tried to defend the newcomer.

"Poor child, yet she's a gentle enough creature."

"And thus quite unsuitable for Barron." Mrs Drummond-Burrell gave a snort of impatience, glancing down for a second at her pearl-embroidered gown with a glow of self-satisfaction. In her view, there wasn't a woman in Almack's that night who looked as well as she did. Fashion may have decreed that the bodice of a dress be low-cut, following the classical pattern of the ancient Greeks, but really, some of those present had gone too far, practically naked, and not caring a whit. "He should have married a strong-minded woman who could manage him, not a chit straight from her governess's side."

"I agree." Lady Castlereagh, *très grande*, and with a mighty opinion of herself, inclined her head, the diamond tiara sparkling under the lights. "But everyone knows why he chose her."

"*Pauvre enfante*." princess Esterhazy giggled. "What must they be like in bed together. Such a fascinating thought, don't you agree?"

The haughty Countess Lieven frowned repressively.

"No, my dear, I do not. For myself, I have long since given up guessing what Charles Barron does in bed. After all, he has lain in so many, hasn't he?"

"She's very rich." Lady Sefton was still sympathetic, for she had incurred several rather heavy debts of late. "And her birth is beyond reproach, you must admit."

"An Austrian count?" Countess Lieven was scornful. "A very obscure one, I can assure you, and I hardly think we need put ourselves out on that account."

"Well, I shall be pleasant to her." The princess was still laughing. "Someone must be, for I'm sure her husband isn't. Why, my dear George, I didn't see you."

Brummell kissed the princess's outstretched hand, his expression wry.

"I'm not sure how to take that, you know. Do I understand that you find me insignificant?"

Princess Esterhazy stood on tip-toe to kiss his cheek.

"You know well enough that isn't so. Now, don't be difficult tonight, for we are having such a splendid time that I absolutely forbid you to spoil things."

Brummell had bowed to each of the patronesses in turn, even the frosty Countess managing a smile for him, for it was unwise to offend the Beau.

"You don't appear to be enjoying it." Brummell was sardonic. "Who, pray, are you talking about, and do I know her?"

"Of course." Lady Castlereagh nodded in the direction of the dancers. "Adelaide Hessen-Holstandt. Such a strange choice for Charles. What can he have been thinking about?"

"His bills." Brummell raised his glass and studied the floor with disdain. "God, what a motley assembly."

The patronesses drew themselves up to their full height, any differences between them forgotten at the Beau's implied criticism. Very few were permitted to enter the hallowed portals of the Club, and here was Brummell suggesting that they had allowed mere commoners to join the élite group.

He saw their indignation and purred inwardly. Although he counted them as his friends, he was in a black mood that night, and had been told of a comment made by Mrs Drummond-Burrell which had not been to his credit. Damned old harridans needed a prod now and then.

"But then, of course," he said finally,

"I realise that you have to suffer some whom you would not normally wish to receive. One of the trials of life, is it not?"

"George, you are impossible!" The princess was dimpling again, never able to sustain ill-temper for long. "Don't be so provoking. Tell us instead what you think of Charles's wife."

"I don't think about her at all." The Beau gave her a cool stare. A pretty enough wench, the Esterhazy belle, with her dark curls and wide innocent-looking eyes, but her claws were as sharp as her companions' when she was put out. "I seldom think of other men's wives."

"Then you are in a class of your own," returned Countess Lieven tartly. "I doubt that there is a man here to-night who wouldn't take another's spouse to his bosom, if he had the chance."

"How astute of you, my dear countess." Brummell was very smooth. "Yet it has taken you rather a long time to reach the obvious. Of course I am in a class of my own. An enviable position, don't you agree?"

He passed on, leaving the ladies torn

between chagrin and satisfaction. It was good that everyone had seen how long the Beau had spent talking to them, but he really could be very trying at times.

Lady Jersey beckoned to one of the bewigged flunkeys nearby.

"Ask Lady Barron to be good enough to come over. Hurry now, before she starts dancing again."

Adelaide Barron's mouth was dry as she approached the formidable group of women who led the London set. She had heard all about them from her maid, a wench with a bottomless chest of gossip and information about society folk, who had regaled her with the history of each of the patronesses, and a warning about their humour.

Adelaide was sure that the flimsy muslin was too revealing, although the ruinously expensive dressmaker had assured her that it was all the rage: she also worried about the rubies which her mother had given her on her marriage to Charles. Surely they were too ostentatious; like shimmering drops of blood.

She shuddered at the thought. At

home, in her father's castle set high on a mountain-side, she had worn the simplest of garb, scarcely a trinket to adorn her plainness. And plain she was, and knew it. Even her maid couldn't make much of the black hair which seemed to spring this way and that, refusing to curl quietly against the jewelled bandeau, and rouge in no way hid the sallowness of her cheeks. She wished she had large blue eyes, for such were greatly admired: instead, the good Lord had endowed her with brown orbs of small size, and sparse lashes. If only her body had made up for what her face lacked it wouldn't have been so bad, but she was thin, like a child, and wholly unexciting.

She felt stripped naked before the battery of eyes looking her over, shaking as she made a brief curtsey to the august dragons who, she had been warned, she must on no account displease.

"Well, my dear." Lady Castlereagh made the first move, managing to conjure up a semblance of a smile. "And how do you like London?"

Adelaide stammered something, aware that she was making a bad impression.

"So different from your home." The Countess Lieven was staring at a brooch the size of a small egg. "Somewhere quite remote, I believe."

"Yes." Adelaide pulled herself together. It was absurd to be so terrified. Charles would think her simple if she let these Gorgons trample over her. "Yes, it is quite different."

"And where is Charles?" Mrs Drummond-Burrell's hard gaze moved round the room. "I see no sign of him."

"I think he has gone to White's." Adelaide's good intentions melted before the wilting stare of her inquisitor. "He will be back soon."

"So I should hope. How quite extrordinary he is."

Adelaide was heartily thankful when the ordeal was over, creeping away to a corner where she could sit and recover her equilibrium. The experience had been almost as bad as her first meeting with Charles Barron, and that had been a moment never to be forgotten.

She could feel the tears hovering as she recalled the occasion. Charles had looked superb. She thought she had never seen a man more comely, nor one who wore his clothes with such panache, but when she had seen the indifference in his eyes, and the grim line of his mouth, her heart had sunk.

Of course, she had had no delusions about the marriage. Her father was not an unkind man, but he had had no time for tact or any nonsense of that sort. No eligible suitor had been found for her in her own country, but word had reached Count Hessen-Holstandt that an Englishman, of impeccable breeding, and shaky fortune, was in the market for a rich wife. Nothing Adelaide had said had made the slightest difference. Her unhappiness and pleadings had resulted in nothing but a cuff round the ear when her father's patience had worn out.

She hung her head, praying that Charles would come for her soon, certain that the dreaded cabal were still discussing her shortcomings.

After an hour, when it was clear that her husband had quite forgotten her, she managed to attract the attention of a servant, who called for her carriage, keeping her head high until she reached her own bedroom, where she threw herself down on the coverlet and sobbed her heart out.

* * *

"I suppose I'd better go home."

Barron yawned, and collected his winnings. It had been a good night, and Dame Fortune had been at his elbow ever since he had arrived at White's. Even when Brummell appeared, complaining of the monotony of the ball at Almack's, Charles had not been reminded of Adelaide. It was only when Alvanley mentioned his wife that Charles remembered his own.

"Come to think of it," he said without enthusiasm. "I should call at Almack's and collect my spouse. How very tedious."

The others nodded. They had well understood Charles's reluctance to marry the Austrian Romany, as people had begun to call her, but they saw that he had had no choice. Too many losses, and too many debts piling up round him: there was nothing else for it but a profitable marriage.

"Saw her, did you, George?" Barron rose, and snapped his fingers at a waiter. "What was she doin' when you left?"

"About to undergo torture at the hands of the martinets." Brummell adjusted his sleeve, frowning at what he thought was a slight crease. "Shouldn't have left her, you know."

"Damn it!" Charles moved to the door, the Beau at his side. "You didn't expect me to spend the night there, prancing round the floor, did you?"

"No, but your wife . . . "

"Confound my wife," replied Charles curtly. "I should never have listened to Argyll. It's his fault I'm in this fix."

"And his fault that you are solvent?" Brummell shrugged. "Can't have it both ways. Try to be kind to the wench. She always looks to me as if she's about to burst into tears."

"She usually is, and if there's one thing I detest it's a weeping, wailing woman. Perhaps half an hour with Lady Jersey and the rest of 'em will make her grow up."

When Barron finally got home, after a fruitless trip to Almack's, he found Adelaide in bed. She sat up abruptly, her face still stained, her nose an unbecoming red.

"Now what's wrong with you?"

Barron had stopped to change into a dressing-gown of deep crimson, reaching the floor. He looked like a god to Adelaide, but his obvious irritation made her shrink back as if he were about to strike her.

"Good God, woman, you're not crying again, surely? Am I so repulsive?"

"No . . . no, sir, but . . . "

"No, Charles! I'm your husband, you know."

"Yes, but . . . "

The silence fell like a leaden pall. Then Charles crossed to the bed and sat on the side, studying Adelaide.

It had been the most appalling mistake. Even the vast dowry she had brought with her did not compensate for the fiasco which was their marriage. During the day she snivelled, and on the nights when he went to her she made him feel as though he were about to rape an innocent infant. Indeed, so great had been her obvious dread that he had never once got as far as pulling the sheets back, far less getting into bed with her.

It was at those times that he found himself thinking of Bess, and her smooth round limbs, laughing eyes, and cloud of red-gold hair which fell to her shoulders and made him catch his breath. Love with Bess was totally fulfilling: no *affaire* he had had before or since had given him such satisfaction.

And it wasn't only that he missed her generous, wonderful loving. For once in his life Charles Barron was feeling guilty, and he didn't like it. He even found himself wondering whether the child had been a boy or a girl, until he told himself not to be a fool, and thrust such pointless thoughts away.

Bess had gone out of his life. Instead, he had Adelaide. His lips thinned. What a price to get one's debtors off one's back: still, it had had to be faced.

He put out one hand and touched Adelaide's cheek, ignoring her instinctive withdrawal.

"You may not think much of me," he

said after a moment, "but since we've got to spend a lifetime together, you'd better get used to me, don't you think?"

He drew the shift down to her waist, and could almost count her ribs. It made him feel sick. A woman should be soft to touch, with yielding flesh, and skin which felt like satin, not a mass of bones.

When he put an arm round her she went as rigid as a pole, and he lost his temper completely.

As he ranted and raved at her, listing her faults and failings, pouring biting scorn on her appearance, Adelaide wept anew. Nothing he said was untrue, and that made it worse. She wanted to love him, and be loved by him, but she didn't know how. Neither her mother nor her father had thought to tell her what to expect of the marriage-bed, and the servants at home hardly spoke to her. Her ignorance was abysmal, and she was totally unaware that such a thing as sexual play existed.

Charles terrified her, and so did his demands. She couldn't respond, and his consequent fury made things worse.

Finally, his rage spent, he handed her a kerchief.

"Blow your nose, for pity's sake."

She obeyed, eyes fixed on him, wondering what he was going to do next. She prayed that he would go away to his dressing-room adjoining the bedroom, but he didn't.

"You'll have to get used to it, you know. I shall need a son."

She gulped.

"I . . . . . . know, but . . . I . . . "

He was torn between impatience and a new kind of pity he hadn't felt before. It was obvious that Adelaide hated the thought of intercourse. She had none of the natural instincts which Bess had had. Bess had said that she was a virgin, and he had found that she had been speaking the truth, but she needed no encouragement. Love came to her as naturally as breathing, and her obvious enjoyment had made his own the greater. He wondered why he kept thinking about Bess, and resolutely turned back to Adelaide.

"You'll get used to the notion." He was almost gentle for once. "Don't fight me. Try to . . . well . . . try to . . . ”

He gave up. How was it possible to take a woman when she was watching one as a rabbit watches a stoat? How to move on to passion when her eyes were puffed up and pink? How to arouse desire when her body was stiff with terror?

“Another time,” he said wearily, and rose from the bed. “For heaven’s sake stop crying! Do you never do anything else?”

When he had gone, Adelaide quickly covered herself, the sheet held tight about her, just in case he changed his mind and came back. She had seen the distaste in him, fleeting though it had been, and shrivelled inside. She didn’t blame Charles. There was nothing about her body to appeal to him. What she despised was her own weakness; loathed her lack of spirit, and mourned inwardly, because she didn’t know how to give Charles what he wanted.

She lay awake most of the night, thinking about him, knowing that in some odd way she wanted him to make love to her, yet knowing, equally, that she was quite unable to tell him so, either by word or gesture.

Then she made herself a promise. Next time, she would be all that he wanted her to be. She wouldn't grizzle or draw away from his touch. She would learn, if he would teach her, and then perhaps he would stop looking at her as if he wished her in Hades.

When at last her eyes closed there was new moisture on her lashes. Promises were all very well, but ignorance was another thing. Who would shew her how to please a man, if Charles wouldn't, and, if she ever learned, would it be too late?

3

IT was six weeks before Bess could get out of bed. She had tried earlier, but her shaking legs would not bear her, and Fred had had to lift her back on to the lumpy mattress, scolding her for her impatience.

"You've got to rest," he had said, trying to be firm, knowing he merely sounded apologetic. "Work'll have to wait, lass. You're not well enough yet."

"Can't let things slide." Bess knew Fred was right, but the house wouldn't run itself. It needed her firm hand on things to keep it going. "What did we take last night?"

When he had told her, Bess had groaned.

"Not enough." She bit her lip. "We'll be ruined. Tell those girls downstairs to buck their ideas up. And what about the cleanin'? Who's doin' that?"

"Me and Miss Cotter. Mr Burnham gives an 'and now and then. Do stop worrin'. Jest get yerself strong; that's all that matters."

And with that Bess had had to be content, but one day when she woke up, she felt different. The terrible weakness had gone, and there was an odd sensation running through her, as if new life were flowing back into her veins.

She threw the bedclothes aside and put an exploratory foot on to the worn rug. When nothing happened she risked the second foot, standing at last without trembling, or feeling the dread faintness.

In the corner of their room was a long mirror. It had been a present from Miss Cotter, who had assured Bess that she had no further need of it. Bess was sure that was a lie, but she loved the looking-glass, for it had a surround of gilded wood, with cherubs and vine leaves in each corner. It was a touch of pure luxury in an otherwise drab world.

When she approached the mirror Bess stopped dead, her eyes registering a sight which she couldn't believe. All the flesh seemed to have melted from her, and her round rosy face was now thin and pale.

For a second or two she just stared

at her image, shocked at first, but then wonderingly. Despite the cold January day she tore her shift off, so that she could see more clearly what the fever had done, running doubtful fingers over her sleek flanks and thighs. The waist could have been spanned by a man's hands; her breasts were small and perfectly rounded.

She moved nearer, peering at her face. No longer full, but the bones were faultless, and she hardly recognised herself. Her green eyes looked larger, and the faint shadows beneath them made them mysterious.

She began to smile, reaching for a pair of scissors. The mass of tumbled waves and curls was wrong. All right for Covent Garden, but that wasn't how the ladies of the *beau monde* wore their locks.

Some instinct told her how to snip away to achieve what she wanted, cropping ruthlessly until her head was covered with short, feathery curls, left deliberately dishevelled, *à la* Titus.

When she put on her dress it was laughable, hanging like a sack on her slender body, and she clapped her hands in delight at what she saw.

It was an adventure to descend the stairs, and she was anxious to watch Fred's face when he saw the new woman she had become, but Fred was nowhere about.

She tried one room and then the next. They were empty, for business did not begin until the evening. Empty, that is, save for one. Bess stood in the doorway and stared at the two girls in the bed. They weren't resting, after a long night's work. They were locked in a tight embrace, mouth to mouth, legs entwined.

It did not shock Bess. She'd met most kinds of perversion in her day, but she'd never let a whiff of the unnatural soil her house.

"Get out, you dirty bitches," she said clearly, her voice a rasp. "I'll have none of that 'ere. Get out, the pair of you, and don't come back. Go to old Mother Grosse's, if you want that sort o' thing, you . . . "

They fled as her invective beat into their ears, and when she heard the clatter of their boots on the stairs she stripped the bedclothes off in disgust. Things had got out of hand during her illness; it was high time she took control again.

In the kitchen Miss Cotter was trying to make a pie, her face flushed, her grey hair flecked with flour.

"Lor'." Bess's ire was gone. "What you doin' then? That stuff's for eatin', you know, not for powderin' a wig."

"Oh, Mrs Walton, I'm so sorry." Christine was nearly in tears. "I know that I am the most wasteful creature in the world, and you do well to scold me, but, you see, I never learned to cook, and . . . oh, I am so sorry!"

"You old silly." Bess laughed and put an affectionate arm round the quivering seamstress. "Well, I do declare you're shakin', and all over a pie. Come on, I've other things for you to do. Notice somethin' different about me, do you?"

Christine wiped her hands on her apron, Bess's gesture driving away her fears, looking at Bess properly for the first time since she had entered the room.

The silence went on so long that Bess grew impatient.

"Well? Don't you see nothin' then?"

Christine nodded, finding her voice with difficulty.

"Oh yes I do. Mrs Walton, you are beautiful! Oh, you really are beautiful!"

Bess threw back her head and laughed.

"Never get a better compliment than that, I guess. Lost some weight, 'aven't I? This dress don't fit me no more. I look a proper fright in it. You'll 'ave to make me something new, Miss Cotter, and that's a fact."

"I will!" Christine's eyes lit up. "Oh, I shall so enjoy that, but meanwhile I think I can find something more to your size. A gown which was ordered and never collected. I'll get it straight away. And Mrs Walton."

"Yes?"

"It is so good to see you up and about again. You don't know how worried we were."

Bess grinned.

"Not as worried as me, luv, but thanks. It's good to be on me feet again."

Half an hour later the two women were back in Bess's bedroom, the unfortunate pie completely forgotten. The dress was of white sarcenet, trimmed with lace, a low decolletage drawn into position by a narrow ribbon, *en coulisse*. It clung lovingly to Bess's body, falling to the ground in simple folds, fitting her as if measured especially for her.

Miss Cotter had found some rouge, touching Bess's cheeks very lightly to dispel the pallor, slipping a rose-tinted ribbon amongst the short locks. The colours should have warred with each other, but they didn't, and Bess gazed at herself in wonder.

"Oh yes, you are lovely." Miss Cotter stepped back to admire her handiwork. "I thought so before, but now . . . well . . . there are no words to describe how you look."

Bess was silent. The seamstress was right. Bess had no false modesty, and the woman looking back at her from the glass was breathtaking, but it wasn't enough.

"Miss Cotter," she said finally, "I'll 'ave more gowns like this; three or four, and trimmed fashionable like." She paused again. "But just lookin' right ain't enough, is it? Got to sound right too, and behave right, what's more."

Miss Cotter nodded, not sure what was coming next. It had been a morning of such surprises, that anything could happen.

"I want you to teach me to talk proper," said Bess. "Bess Walton is dead, Miss Christine. It's Elizabeth now, and Elizabeth must know 'ow to say the right thing, and which fork and knife to use. You know, all those things what the gentry do. I want to learn. I'll pay you, of course, but you'll 'ave to be quick about it, 'cos I've wasted enough time as it is."

"I don't need payment." Christine was beaming. "What fun it will be. Dear Mrs Walton, I'll gladly teach you."

"And I'll pay," repeated Bess firmly. "That's only right. Now where's that Mr Burnham gone?"

"Out, I think. Why?"

"Got to 'ave a bit o' education too, ain't I? Can't be a lady an' ignorant. 'E'll 'ave to school me some."

"I'm sure he will be delighted." Christine broke off, looking doubtful for the first time. "But will you be able to do it all? I mean, if you keep this house going, and have so very much to learn . . . oh! I'm so sorry, dear Mrs Walton, I didn't mean to imply . . . "

Bess chuckled.

"I knows, but yer right. I'm a low-born demi-rep what's got to turn into a fine lady, and, yes, I know it'll be'ard, but I don't care."

"But you've been so ill."

"I'm better now. Fit as a fiddle. Get 'old of Mr Burnham, there's a dear. Tell 'im I wants to talk to 'im."

The metamorphosis of Bess Hathaway to Mrs Elizabeth Walton took six months. During that time, Bess worked so hard that Fred was in despair. The shock of finding so ravishing a creature as his wife had become had been bad enough. Now, she spoke softly, not dropping her aitches, and so pernickety at table that he felt like a clod. He begged her not to wear herself out, but she only smiled.

"Fred, I have a lot of time to make up."

"I know, but . . . "

"Please do not worry about me. This place is paying so well that I think in a week or two we can look about for a better establishment."

"Leave 'ere!" Fred was aghast. "But, Bess . . ."

"Elizabeth."

"Sorry." He coloured. He found it difficult to remember to call her by her new name, knowing that he would always think of her as Bess in his heart. "But why should we move?"

"Because this is a slum, and I don't belong here any more."

She was cool and very assured.

"I shall seek a place in the Strand, and later, a better district still. Don't concern yourself, Fred, I'll see to it all."

She didn't notice the slump of his shoulders as she left him, nor the dread in his eyes. He knew he was going to lose her; it was as plain to him as the nose on his face. Not that she had been anything but kindly, still accepting him in her bed as before, but their love-making was no longer pleasurable. Passion, there had never been, but comfort, yes. Now that was gone. Fred was almost afraid to touch her, for she seemed like a goddess to him, and his fearful fumblings beneath the sheets was a sorry thing for both of them.

True to her word Bess found her house in the Strand, and called in builders to put right the timbers and bricks, furnishing it with excellent taste, helped by Miss Cotter.

Bess had allotted small rooms to her mentors, Christine and Mr Burnham, and the lessons in deportment, etiquette, history, politics, music and dancing went on in between the rush and bustle of running the brothel.

Fred hated it. By common consent, and with no words spoken on the subject, he now had his own room in the basement, but, alone at night, he longed to be back in Covent Garden, with plump, cheerful Bess giving him a hearty buss or two which had made his toes tingle.

Bess's star was in the ascent. Everything she touched was successful, and her business flourished. She had bought herself a few jewels, and now went to a smarter dressmaker to have her gowns made. Twice a week a woman came in to wash her hair and coax it into the shining disorder which turned men's heads wherever she went, and she had even purchased a phaeton and two fine horses, which were stabled at the side of her new house.

But real fortune struck when Bess met Anthony Carter, a rich banker, who took an instant fancy to her. It was Carter who taught her to gamble, and encouraged her to use part of her premises for the playing of faro, macao and other games of chance. He knew nothing about her past, and had accepted her as she was: an elegant, fashionable beauty, with a remarkable intelligence, who could discuss subjects which most women would have known nothing about.

Steadfastly Bess refused to sleep with Carter, thus keeping him dangling and hopeful. It was not out of loyalty to Fred that she had spurned the banker, nor that she had grown sexually cold. She had no intention of gaining a reputation for promiscuousness, unless the rewards were really worth it, and she contented herself with flirting gently with the besotted Carter, her eyes making promises she had no intention of keeping.

In his basement room, Fred grew

sadder and sadder. Bess never came to him now, and when they encountered each other, which wasn't often, they were almost like strangers. Bess was always pleasant, plying him with gifts and money, which he didn't want. All he wanted was Bess, and she had long gone.

By December 1808 she had accumulated sufficient funds to cut the banker out of her life, and shewed no compunction in the doing. Instead of worrying about him, she bought a fashionable mansion in Kensington which was to be her home and nothing more. She now had three brothels, all successful, but it was time to put distance between them and herself.

Now, her wardrobes bulged with the latest gowns and mantles, her jewel-case full of diamonds, rubies, pearls and emeralds, some which Carter had pressed upon her, others which she had bought herself.

She went to all the smart places, admired by every man, and hated by every woman, for, as her self-assurance blossomed, so did her beauty. There were whispers about where such a divine creature had come from, for no one could discover a thing about her past life, but the probing did not last for long. The witty, exquisite Elizabeth Walton was the talk of the town, and even the grandest of hostesses were glad to include her amongst their guests.

Everyone assumed that she was a widow, for she never spoke of her husband, and Fred kept well out of the way, until one day, when Bess was dressing for dinner, he ventured into her room.

She was surprised, for he hadn't sought her out for so long. She had a fleeting stab of concern, lest he had come to remind her that she was his wife, and the thought that she might have to reject him worried her. But the concern on this score didn't last for long.

"You want to buy a farm?" She was incredulous, staring at Fred as he shuffled his large feet on the thick pile of the carpet. "My dear, whatever for? No one lives on a farm."

"Some do." He was a bit afraid of her, and her scorn, but this was so important to him that he had to stand up to her. “Those what sow and harvest the wheat, and milk the cows, and such like.”

“Well, yes, but . . . ”

“I was brought up in the country. I told you that when . . . ”

Bess turned her head slowly to look in the mirror, seeing the rose lips, green eyes beneath darkened lashes, the fragile hollows in the cheeks.

She hadn’t always looked like that. Once, and not so long ago, she had been dirty and fat and afraid, but Fred hadn’t cared. He had married her, fleas and all, to give Charles Barron’s child a name. Charles. Bess touched the pearl necklace round her slender throat with fingers which weren’t quite steady.

Charles had been in Brighton for several months, and so she had seen nothing of him as she moved from one drawing-room to the next, but she had been told that he was returning next week, and it was inevitable that they would meet. Determinedly she shut thoughts of Barron out of her mind and looked back at Fred.

“Yes, so you did. I’ve disappointed

you, haven't I? I'm not the woman you wanted me to be."

"No, no!" His protest was swift, his eyes blurring. "No, Bess . . . I mean Elizabeth, you haven't done no such thing. You're so beautiful, and I'm the proudest man in the land, but you must see there's no place for me 'ere. Can't sit for ever in that room down there."

"You didn't have to stay there." She frowned slightly. "Why do you sit there night after night, when you could be upstairs with the rest of us?"

He managed a smile, but she could see that his lips were trembling.

"And 'ave people find out yer 'usband's a pot-man, an' not dead at all? No, I couldn't let that 'appen."

Now it was Bess's eyes which were moist, and she got up slowly.

"Oh, Fred, what have I done to you?"

"Nothin', nothin'. You ain't done nothin'. It's just that I want to go back to the fields and 'edgerows where I belong. That's all."

She moved forward, taking his face between her slim fingers.

"Oh, love, forgive me. I didn't mean

to hurt you so. I didn't think what I was doing to you. Everything seemed to happen so quickly, and once it started there seemed no stopping it. I hadn't meant to come so far. All I wanted for us was a better life, but then . . . well . . . "

"Yes, I know." He comforted her, bony hands clasped round her delicate wrists. "Yes, I understand, an' I'm not blamin' you. I'd never blame you, Bess, I mean, Elizabeth."

"Bess." She whispered it, afraid of breaking down. "I'm Bess, and always will be to you. Must you go? I can't bear the thought that I'm driving you away. You married me when no other man would have had a moment's time for me. I owe you so much."

"You owes me nothin'." Fred was terse. "Jest forget that. I didn't marry yer 'cos I were sorry for yer; I loved yer. I still does."

"Oh God!"

Very gently he took her in his arms, afraid of creasing the expensive gown, holding her against him, feeling her tears against his cheek.

"There, there, don't go on so. We're

not partin' forever are we? Now and then, maybe, you'll come and see me on the farm. Saved up a bit, yer know. Tucked away the money you gave me, and I've got a nice little place. That day I said I was goin' to see me cousin . . . well . . . I didn't. Went to Somerset instead, and made the arrangements. Didn't like lyin' ter yer, Bess, but it was summat I 'ad ter do on me own."

"Yes, I know." She raised her head, the tears still trickling down. "I've always done the arranging, haven't I, and never once asked what you thought. I'll miss you. I know I haven't been a proper wife to you for a long time, but I always knew you were here. You may not believe me, but that meant a lot to me."

"I believes you. Now, wipe yer face, or you'll be late. I'll be agoin' next week."

"So soon!"

"Nothin' to wait for."

She closed her eyes.

"No, I suppose not. I'll come and see you; I promise I will."

"Well, see 'ow it goes. You're busy."

"Not too busy to see you." She managed a smile at last, holding his hand. "I must go now, but later, when I get back, shall I come down to you?"

He put his head on one side, taking in each small piece of her as if to tuck it away in his memory where it couldn't be lost. He was almost tempted to accept her offer, for in the last few minutes they had become closer than they'd been for a long time, but there was no point in prolonging the hurt.

"No, Bess," he said quietly. "I'm grateful you asked, but no."

She nodded, the pain inside her so much sharper than she had imagined it would be.

"Perhaps you're right. You were always wiser than me."

"Wouldn't say that, and you knowin' so much."

"Book-learning doesn't mean a thing. That's not wisdom." She couldn't look at him. "Perhaps I shouldn't have . . . "

"Don't go lookin' back." He was firm. "You've done what you've done, now don't go regrettin' it. Well, I must be off. Enjoy yerself; I'll see yer afore I goes."

When the door closed behind him Bess

began to repair the ravages her tears had wrought. She was almost finished when Christine came in. Miss Cotter was now Bess's personal maid, and enjoying every moment of it.

"The carriage is here, Mrs Walton. Why . . . is anything wrong . . . you look . . . "

She was all concern, but Bess waved her away.

"Nothing, nothing." Bess was herself again.

There was not a trace of her inner misery and remorse reflected on her face as she glanced once more in the mirror. The lovely Mrs Walton was about to join Mrs Drummond-Burrell and her guests for dinner, and she was quite determined that not one of them should guess that her heart was near to breaking.

* * *

Charles Barron returned from Brighton four days later. He had had a hectic few months in the company of the Prince of Wales, Brummell, and the Carlton House set, drinking, dicing, and racing his horses as if the hounds of hell were after him.

Because he had lost consistently at the tables, he had also had to call upon his current mistress, Lady Malvern, for financial assistance. She was no beauty, but an expert in the art of erotic love, and exceedingly rich. She had chided Charles for the way he threw his money away, but when he had kissed her, and told her that she was the only woman in the world for him, she had given in.

She knew that he was lying, but it didn't matter: she had long since stopped believing in true love. She adored Barron, and what were diamonds for, if not to sell?

Adelaide was waiting for Barron when he got home. He thought she looked plainer than ever, the mournful eyes exasperating him. She had the unfailing ability to make him feel guilty, despite the fact that it was she who had caused their marriage to be as arrid as a desert. He threw his cane and gloves into a chair, and nodded.

"Well, my dear, I trust that you are well."

Adelaide rose from the dressing-table to receive a brief salute on her cheek.

"Yes thank you."

"You don't look it." He was still short with her. Why didn't she spit her fury at him, as Bess would have done? Why did she cringe in front of him like a whipped cur? And, in God's name, why did he keep thinking of Bess? "You're as scrawny as a pikestaff. Don't you take proper meals?"

"Yes, of course. Really, sir, I am quite well."

He had almost given up trying to make her call him Charles: the effort seemed pointless, since she treated him like a man she had only just met.

Adelaide could see the menacing line of his lips; feel the impatience. It was the same whenever they were together, and her stomach began to churn.

If only she knew what to say to him; how to greet him properly, but she didn't. All she could manage was a stilted phrase, expressing her pleasure that he was home again.

"I swear, George," said Charles a few hours later as he and Brummell made their way to White's, "that I don't know what to do with that wife of mine. She's as lifeless as a dummy, and contrives to make me feel a brute when I do no more than say good-evening."

"Send her to Lady Malvern for lessons." The Beau was perfection in full evening-dress. He thought that he and Robinson had surpassed themselves, for every inch of him was a study in sartorial elegance. "Does she know about Rachel, by the way?"

"I haven't told her." Barron had his own style, and his height and good looks almost overshadowed the Beau's presence. "Someone may have mentioned it to her, of course, but she's far too scared of me to say anything."

"My dear Charles." The Beau's voice was a drawl. "You must indeed be a brute to terrify that poor child so. Why don't you be civil to her for a change?"

"Curse it, I am civil, at least, most of the time. That's the whole trouble. We're both so civil that we scarcely speak."

"Then you'd better remedy that, if you want an heir." Brummell stopped at the Club's entrance. "I'm not an expert on these matters, m'dear fellow; far too many other things to attend to, but even I can see you'll never begat a son, nodding to each other across the room. For pity's sake, what's the matter with you? You've bedded enough women to know what to do. Now, forget it for the moment, I beg you. Frustrated love and cards don't mix, and it's time that you started winning again."

The Prince of Wales had come to White's that night, nodding affably to Charles.

"Back from Brighton, eh? Sometimes think I ought to stay there for good. Further away from my father, don't you know."

"How is his majesty?"

The prince heaved a sigh. He was putting on weight fast, unwanted pounds stretching the coloured waistcoat until it seemed it must burst.

"Mad as a hatter, and as pig-headed as ever."

"I'm sorry to hear it."

"Hm." The prince's pout vanished. "Well, don't let's discuss my father's mental instability to-night. Better things to do, what? How about a game of faro? Wager you a hundred pounds that I beat you in the first game."

Charles got home at two in the morning. He had won five thousand, and was in a good humour. The company had been merry, the wine potent. All he wanted then was his bed.

It was therefore something of a shock to discover that, when he had dismissed his valet at the door, assuring the man he was quite capable of undressing himself, his bed was already occupied.

"Adelaide?"

Charles sobered very quickly, astounded to find his wife sitting bolt upright, a look of terror in her eyes.

"My dear!" He crossed the floor quickly, taking her shaking hands in his. "What is it? What has frightened you?"

She shook her head mutely, and he bared his teeth, the familiar annoyance creeping over him again.

"Something must have done." He tried to control himself. "Otherwise, you would hardly be in my bed, would you, since it is not a place you favour particularly."

She managed to look at him, hypnotised by the beauty of his face. She wanted so much to tell him how handsome she thought him, but the words simply would not come.

"Nothing . . . sir . . . nothing frightened me."

He released her abruptly.

"Then what on earth are you doing here?"

"I had a letter from my father to-day."

"Oh? And it contained bad news?"

"No, no, it wasn't that."

"Then in heaven's name, what? Surely you haven't sat up this late to read me a letter from your father?"

"No, but in it he says . . . "

She couldn't go on, and Barron drew a deep breath.

"Madam, if you have something to tell me, then get it out and be done with it. If not, go to bed, for I'm tired and need my sleep."

She hung her head, unable to bear his obvious dislike of her. Yet she had to tell him sooner or later, and since she had plucked up sufficient courage to come to his room it had better be said.

"My father says I must have a son."

Barron's lips parted.

"He says what!"

"I must have a son . . . children." Adelaide said it very rapidly, still avoiding his eye. "He says I am not doing my duty as a wife, and that . . . "

"What business is it of his?" Barron was curter than ever. "You are my wife, not his."

"I am his daughter."

"That has nothing to do with it."

"He says it has, and he's right." Suddenly, she was bold enough to look at him, the words tumbling out of the prison in which they had been locked for so long. "Yes, he is right. I haven't done my duty as a wife. You see, no one told me how to be one, and when we . . . when you . . . that is. when I . . . well . . . I couldn't! And I'm so sorry, because I do love you so very much, and you're the nicest-looking man I've ever seen."

Barron stared at her for a minute longer: then he began to laugh.

"Oh, my poor child!"

"I'm not a child!"

"Indeed you are, but that can soon be changed." He sat on the side of the bed, still laughing. "I can tell you about love, since no one else has bothered to do so."

Her cheeks were warm, and she didn't like him making fun of her, but the die was cast now.

"I would be most grateful. I will try to be a diligent pupil."

"Good God, girl, we're not going to embark upon a history lesson."

"I know that, but . . ."

Charles's amusement died, and he looked at his wife thoughtfully. The pinkness in her cheeks made her eyes look brighter, and in the candlelight the fact that she was not fashionably blonde and ethereally pale didn't seem to matter quite so much. He felt an unexpected twinge of pity. What cruelty parents inflicted on their offspring. What had the girl's mother been thinking about to send her to England to wed without giving her a single word of advice?

Of course, Bess had needed no advice. He frowned, cursing to himself because her name kept coming back to him, just as the vision of her face was never far from his mind. Again he wondered what had happened to her and where she was now. Then he forced her away, as he had done so many times before, concentrating on Adelaide and her worried expression.

"You'll have to take your dressing-gown off," he said gently. "I'll be back in a while. Don't be alarmed. I never eat my wives."

Fifteen minutes later he returned to find that the pink in Adelaide's cheeks had turned to scarlet, and that she was hugging the sheet about her as if life itself depended on it.

At first he simply talked to her, softly and comfortingly. Then, when some of her rigidity had gone, he touched her hand, emboldened to run his fingers up her arm when she didn't draw back.

"Don't be afraid," he whispered, and blew out the light. "I'm told I'm rather good at this. I may lose at the tables now and then, but never in bed."

She gave a small giggle, and he relaxed. The first hurdle was over at least. Laughter was a good companion when making love; he and Bess had laughed a lot. As he drew the sheet down, he wondered once more why he didn't recall other women as he recalled Bess. He never remembered Rachel Malvern, unless he was actually with her, and as for the rest of his mistresses, he'd almost forgotten their names.

"Don't be afraid," he repeated, and held the thin, trembling body against his own. "It really isn't so bad, you know. Indeed, you may even grow to enjoy it. Come, Adelaide, give me a kiss, and let's see how we get on after that."

4

BESS was at a ball with the Earl of Crayford when the news of Fred's death came. Once Fred had left London, Bess let slip the fact that her husband was alive but an invalid. He had to remain in the country, she told a notable gossip, knowing it would be all round London by the morning. His health wouldn't stand up to the bad humours of London: he needed fresh air and rest.

He'd been gone for two months, but, despite her promise, she'd not yet been to Somerset to see the farm. There were so many other things to do; so many calls upon her time. One day, she had assured herself, she would go. Perhaps next week, or the one after that.

When Bess heard that Christine Cotter was waiting in the ante-room to speak to her, she knew at once that something was seriously wrong. Christine, that most perfect instructress in etiquette, would never have intruded on such an occasion unless it had been essential.

"Thomas, will you forgive me? My maid has an urgent message for me."

"Of course, m'dear, but don't be long. So dull, unless you're here."

The earl was as fat as the Prince of Wales, but a good-natured man, well endowed with lands and money. His infatuation with Mrs Walton was accepted by everyone, no one doubting that she was his mistress. Only Bess, and the longing nobleman, knew how wrong they were.

"Christine? What is it? My dear, you are as white as a sheet! What's the matter?"

Miss Cotter was trembling, not knowing how to begin.

"Well?" Anxiety made Bess sharper than she had meant to be. "Don't stand there and make me guess! What's wrong?"

"I . . . forgive me . . . I didn't mean to . . . I didn't know what to do. When the message came from Somerset . . ."

"Fred!"

Bess was as bleached as Christine now,

her eyes darkening with fear.

"Fred! What's happened to him? Is he ill?"

She knew at once that it was something worse, for Christine's head was bent. She controlled the wild desire to burst into tears, and to call for Fred, who had loved her so much, and to whom she had given so little.

"How did he die?"

She asked it quietly, all her dread rigidly under control.

"A bull." Christine was whispering. "He was gored . . . they tried to save him, but it was too late."

"Did he die at once?" Bess's hands were gripped at her side, silently begging Miss Cotter to say yes. "It was instant, wasn't it?"

"I . . . I . . . expect so."

Bess stifled the moan.

"For God's sake don't lie to me now; not about this. He didn't die at once, did he? What did they say?"

"Please, Mrs Walton, don't upset yourself. I know they would have done everything they could to ease the pain until . . . "

"How long?"

"A few hours they said."

"A few hours." Bess repeated it dully, the dreadful truth spreading through her body like a fever. "He lived for a few hours, and I wasn't there."

"You didn't know!" Miss Cotter caught Bess's hand. "Oh, my dear, don't blame yourself, for it was nothing that you did. You didn't know."

"I would have known, if I'd been where a wife belonged: by his side."

Bess pulled herself together, the agony tucked in where no one else could see it.

"Thank you for coming. I must go back now, but tomorrow we'll make all the arrangements."

Make the arrangements! It was always she who made the arrangements. Only once had Fred thrown off the yoke of her efficiency and made his own plans. Just once, and it had killed him.

"Bad news, m'dear?" The earl thought Bess seemed different. No longer gay and carefree as she had been when she had left him. "What is it? Tell me; it'll help."

"I doubt it." She allowed herself to be helped to a chair, accepting brandy. "My husband is dead."

"I see." Thomas forced himself to look grave, and not to let his relief show. "Well, natural enough that you should be saddened, but he was an invalid, wasn't he? Probably glad to be out of his misery, poor devil."

Bess wanted to scream at Thomas to be quiet. To shriek aloud, and say that Fred had been a hardy man, ailing nothing, and that he had lain in unbelievable pain for hours before death had come to end his torment. But all she said was:

"Yes, when the end came, I expect he was glad."

"Not the right time to speak of this, I know. Poor taste, some might say, but don't mean it that way."

"What?"

She looked at the earl vaguely, having no idea what he was talking about.

"The time and place; not the best."

"Time and place for what?"

"To ask you to marry me." He seemed surprised that she was puzzled. "You know how I feel about you, Elizabeth.

Understood why you wouldn't be my mistress whilst your husband lived; respect you for it too. Now he's gone, there's nothing to stop us, is there?"

Bess didn't know whether to laugh or cry. Either was dangerous, for each could turn to hysteria. Her first instinct was to get up and walk away, but something stopped her.

Fred was dead, so that he couldn't be hurt any more. Whatever she did, Fred was beyond suffering now. She had heard that Charles Barron had returned to the capital for only a short while, and had, thereafter, taken his young wife back to Brighton. Yet only yesterday she had learned that they were due back in London within the week.

A meeting between Charles and herself had only been postponed because of his absences from London. Now he was returning nothing could stop them encountering each other, for they moved in the same circles.

Bess was as hard as stone. As a countess, she would outrank Charles's wife. Whatever she decided to do to punish Charles, and such thoughts had never left her, it would be easier to achieve as Thomas's wife. Her determination had grown the stronger when it had been whispered the second trip to Brighton was a postponed honeymoon between Barron and the Austrian Romany. Bess had hated his mistresses, known or unknown, but she had a scalding loathing of Adelaide, for she was Charles's wife.

She let the iron go out of her soul for a while, clinging to the earl's hand, and forcing a tear. It was hard to do, for she couldn't cry openly for Fred. That would come later, when she was alone.

"I hadn't thought, sir, that you would want me as your wife. I swear I am quite overcome."

"Nonsense." Thomas patted her cheek. "Don't gull me, Elizabeth. You know you've wound me round your little finger these past months, and the honour's mine. Is it yes, then?"

"Yes, Thomas," she replied demurely. "There is nothing that I would like better than to be yours."

"Then a kiss to seal the bargain, and after that champagne. I promise you we'll swim in the stuff to-night, Bess."

"No!"

"Eh?" The earl looked blank. "What's wrong with champagne?"

"Don't call me that."

"What?"

"Bess. I don't like it." The sharpness melted again. She mustn't antagonize Thomas. "Forgive me, dearest, I know I sounded like a scold, but it is a name I hate. I do so much prefer Elizabeth."

The earl looked relieved. One was never sure with women.

"Then Elizabeth it shall be, and death to those who call you otherwise. God, I'm the luckiest man in the world! Kiss me, my love, and be damned to those who see us."

⋆ ⋆ ⋆

As Thomas's wife, Elizabeth was received everywhere, even the prince felt giddy when he looked into the clear emerald eyes of the slender countess.

"You are a lucky devil, Thomas," he said, after a concert at Carlton House. "Can't for the life of me see why you should have found favour with such an enchantress, can you, George?"

Brummell raised his eye-glass and studied the countess with care.

"No, sir, I'm bound to say I can't. A veritable goddess. What did you do, Thomas? Bewitch her?"

"I swear I never did a thing." The earl was as contented as a well-fed cat. Elizabeth had made him the envy of all his friends, and in bed she was the most exciting thing he had ever encountered, her appetite for love a complete contrast to the cool exterior she presented to the world. "Not a thing. Just said I wanted her."

"Don't we all?" murmured Brummell. "Ah, sir, here's Charles at last. I thought that he and the unfortunate Adelaide had taken up permanent residence in Brighton, they've been so long there."

"Could do worse." The prince tossed off another glass of claret. "Splendid place, Brighton, and a decent way away from my family. Lot to be said for it. Charles, m'dear fellow. Welcome back."

Barron made a graceful bow, stepping aside to allow Adelaide to curtsey to the prince. Brummell's eyes narrowed faintly.

The girl looked positively radiant. The eyes were sparkling, the lips redder than he had remembered, and a touch of rouge had quite dimmed the yellowish tinge of her complexion. Even her body seemed to have filled out, the low-cut gown of muslin, trimmed with seed pearls, making much of a small bosom.

He let his gaze move on to Charles. A quite remarkable man. Never knew what he'd be up to next.

The prince saw Bess coming towards them.

"Thomas, you must introduce your bride to Charles and Lady Barron. Weren't here for the weddin', you know. Fact is, don't think Charles has ever met Elizabeth, have you?"

"Elizabeth?" Charles cocked an eyebrow. "Have I missed something important during my absence?"

"Indeed you have." The prince chuckled, and took another glass from a passing waiter. "Loveliest thing you ever saw came into our midst not long after you'd gone to Brighton for the first time. Must have heard of her though: Elizabeth Walton."

"Yes." Barron nodded. "Word did reach me of the divine Mrs Walton, but we haven't met."

"Too late." The prince sobered as he caught Adelaide watching him. "That is, she's Thomas's wife now, you see, and here she is. Well, my dear, come and meet an old friend of mine, Sir Charles Barron, and his wife, Adelaide. Charles, the Countess of Crayford."

Charles turned casually, prepared to make another bow, and found himself face to face with Bess. It was as if something had struck him hard on the back of the neck, making his head pound, and his heart race like one of his own greys.

He couldn't believe his eyes, or what the prince was saying, yet under the costly gown and ropes of matchless pearls he could see it was the old Bess. Not as she had been, for the closely curled head was a long way from the tangle of gold, shot with red, which he had insisted she wash before they went to bed together. Not, indeed, as she had been, for she was so slim that it seemed a mere puff of wind might blow her away.

For once in his life Barron was bereft of words. He could only stare, and wait for Bess to make the first move.

For Bess's part the shock had been just as great. Although it was a meeting which she had promised herself for a long time, now that he was here, within inches of her, she felt the same savage jolt that Charles himself was experiencing. She had forgotten how tall he was: how marvellous he was to look at. She had thought herself proof against those lazy eyes under bored lids, but she had been wrong.

She wanted him as much now as she had done in that sordid room in Covent Garden. Her body ached for him, and only iron self-control stopped her from putting her arms round his neck and pulling his mouth down to meet hers. Even the remembrance of his advice to go whoring again once her bastard had been born didn't help at that moment. Her whole being was filled with desire for him, and she knew that it was a lust which must be stifled quickly.

"Sir Charles, Lady Adelaide." She was

very distant. "I trust you found Brighton to your taste."

"Thank you, yes." Charles finally regained his composure. "A remarkably bracing atmosphere. I am sorry I was not here for your wedding."

"Are you?" Her eyes were like pieces of glass. "How strange. We managed very well without you."

The frost in the air was so apparent that the prince and Brummell exchanged a quick look. Odd that Elizabeth was so cold to Charles, since they'd never seen each other before. The prince didn't like unpleasantness, and withdrew hastily, the Beau sauntering after him.

"Thomas, I congratulate you. I had heard of your good fortune, of course, but had never expected to find the gods had favoured you so."

Adelaide's excitement at returning to London had faded. Her high spirits were sagging as she met the icy stare of the countess. She couldn't imagine what she had done to upset the earl's wife, but it was clear that she was being received with very little favour.

"H . . . have you been to Brighton?"

Adelaide ventured the question into what promised to be the most difficult of silences. "You would like it, I'm sure."

"Naturally I have been there." Bess looked the girl over slowly from the tip of silken slippers to the hurt brown eyes. "What an odd question."

Charles's lips compressed. The shattering surprise was over, and now quick anger took its place. Bess, who had come up from the gutter to wed an earl, was deliberately snubbing Adelaide, and half society was watching. He said tightly:

"I don't find it odd. Not everyone knows Brighton. Why, I once knew a girl who'd never been further south than Southwark."

Bess's face was a shade whiter, her eyes a fraction more glacial. She was picturing the stupid, dark-skinned girl with the frightened air lying next to Charles in bed, their flesh touching. It made her long to hurt Adelaide as hard as possible.

"Really, sir, what peculiar people you must know." Another flicker of contempt over Adelaide, the beautiful mouth curling slightly. "Yes, indeed, most peculiar. Thomas, shall we go? I find this conversation rather banal."

She swept away, leaving Barron stiff with fury. Even Thomas's apologetic look did not compensate for the tears in Adelaide's eyes, and Charles said softly:

"Don't cry. Don't let her see that she has hurt you. Don't ever let anyone know that they can hurt you, for you place too dangerous a weapon in their hands. Now come, we shall dance."

"I . . . would rather go home."

"So would I, but we shall stay here. No one is going to say that Elizabeth Merchant drove us away."

"Merchant?"

"It is Thomas's family name. Hers was something quite different, a long time ago."

She looked up, wanting to ask what he meant, but his expression was so remote that she did not dare.

After a while, Charles left Adelaide with Lady Sefton and her companions and sent a flunkey with a message to Bess. It was hastily written, but it served its purpose, for within five minutes Bess closed the door of the ante-room behind her.

"Well?" She kept her chin up, but her mouth was as dry as dust. "Why do you want to see me?"

"Come, Bess, why shouldn't I want to see you?"

"Don't call me that!" Anger lent her courage. "My name is Elizabeth, but I have not given you permission to address me so."

"Bess Hathaway." He drove the rapier in without mercy. "Whore, bawd, strumpet! You have just insulted my wife in public, and I won't have it."

He struck her hard across the face, ignoring her cry of pain.

"You will be civil to Adelaide, and when you next meet her you will apologise."

"Apologise!" Bess was nursing her sore cheek. "I most certainly will not. How dare you lay hands on me? When my husband finds out . . . "

" . . . what you are, he'll be done with you. Hold your tongue, and listen to me."

"I will not! I'm going now, so do not try to stop me."

Charles caught her by the shoulders

and shook her so hard that the diamond-trimmed combs fell from her hair.

"Stop talking, and listen. You will apologise to my wife, but more than that."

She struggled to free herself, but she was no longer the strong, brawny Bess who could hold her own in any fight, and Charles had always had a grip of iron.

"More? Let me go, sir, let me go! What more? I don't know what you're talking about."

"Then I'll explain. If I let you go, will you stand still? If you don't, I'll give you another box round the ears."

"Oh! You are . . . quite insufferable. No man has ever treated me so roughly before."

"Don't be so absurd." His hands dropped to his sides. "You forget to whom you are speaking. Your father whipped you regularly; you told me so yourself, and you got a hiding or two from me, if you remember."

"God, how I detest you, Charles Barron! I loathe you more than I've ever loathed anyone in my life."

"Good. Hate is said to be very close

to love, and we are going to love again, Bess."

"What!" She stopped for a second, startled by his words. "What are you saying?"

"That we shall become lovers again."

"You are mad! How could we? Besides, I would rather die than sleep with you."

"Death is not the alternative." He was smiling at her, no glimmer of humour in his half-closed eyes. "The option is exposure, Bess, my girl. In two days, at midnight, you will meet me in the house where I first took you. I will make the necessary arrangements."

The insult was not lost on her: he thought her place was in the slums of Covent Garden, not here, in the company of the prince and other nobility.

"You are mad. I was right: you are out of your mind."

"I have never felt so sane."

"I shall not come."

"Then I shall tell Thomas, and the world, who you are."

"They wouldn't believe you."

"I could prove it, and you know it. You're beaten; admit it."

"I shall do no such thing! What proof could you give?"

"There are many kinds. For example, are all your relatives dead? Your father, your mother?"

She grew quieter.

"No, but they wouldn't know me now."

"I knew you."

"That's different."

"Not in the least." He had started to enjoy himself. "A mother would scarcely fail to recognise her own daughter, even if the daughter had shed a good deal of weight and cut her hair."

"She wouldn't give me away."

"She would, if I paid her enough."

"You are the most unspeakable man I've ever known." Bess's voice was very low. "I'll never rest until I've paid you back for every last hurt you've done me."

"Your plans will have to be postponed," he returned blandly. "Two days hence, and be sure to be there, for I mean what I say. You will become my mistress, or the whole of London shall know the Countess of Crayford for the low-born slut she really is. Good-night, and remember to apologise to Adelaide."

He let her go, picking up the combs and laying them on a side-table. He doubted if Bess would express sorrow to Adelaide that night, but she would in time; he'd see to that.

Meanwhile, in two days he would see Bess again. The thought of her, which had never left him, would be a reality once more. Not the over-plump, grubby Bess he'd known, but a woman so breathtakingly desirable that he had felt weak, even as he bullied her.

She wouldn't risk losing all that she had fought for, simply to avoid bedding with him. He felt a curious warmth inside him: a desire he had not felt for some time. Two days, and they would be together again. He smiled, and went off to find Adelaide, and to rescue her from Lady Jersey and her friends.

* * *

Bess was glad that Thomas had drunk too much wine that night, for to keep up the pretence of being a dutiful wife would have been an impossibility.

All she could think of was Charles. It was fortunate that no one had noticed the redness of her cheek, nor the fact that she had left the assembly rather too rapidly.

She lay in bed, staring into the darkness, Thomas's thunderous snores assailing her from the direction of his dressing-room.

She had always known she and Charles would meet again: that had been part of her plan. What she had not envisaged was that he would gain the upper hand. In her dreams it was always she who held the whip over him; never he who twisted the crop round to strike at her.

She thought about their intended meeting, and shivered. It was not fear nor resentment, and she knew it. It was pure, unadulterated longing for him; a terrible lust, which all the months apart and all the insults couldn't cure.

She would have to be very strong, and never let him see how she felt about him, for then his hold on her would be the tighter. She would go through with it, for, as Charles had said, she had no choice, but he must never know that she craved for the touch of his hand on her body, and the feel of his strength by her side.

"Damn you, Charles Barron," she said aloud, for Thomas was past hearing anything. "Damn you ten thousand times. Oh! How I do abominate you!"

* * *

Whilst Bess lay in bed cursing, Charles himself was at White's, playing cards for high stakes.

At three o'clock in the morning Brummell was moved to say:

"Charles, for heaven's sake! That's another ten thousand you've lost."

"Then it behoves me to win at least twenty thousand with my next hand, doesn't it?"

Barron was slightly drunk. He couldn't remember how many glasses he'd downed, nor whether the contents was brandy, rum, madeira, champagne, or a mixture of the lot. Furthermore, he didn't care.

The sight of Bess Hathaway, whatever her true title was now, had affected him more than he had believed possible. He prided himself on the fact that he could conduct discreet *affaires* with any woman in the land and remain emotionally unmoved by the experience.

It had annoyed him in the past that he had caught himself thinking about Bess, when anyone with a grain of common sense would have dismissed the grubby urchin from his mind long since. That she had disturbed the tranquillity of his life had been bad enough: that she had now entered his life again and turned his world upside down was unforgivable.

He had hardly been able to believe his eyes. That small, proud head, dressed with exquisite, calculated disorder: the green eyes so cold and bright that they made her jewels seem almost dull by comparison: the perfection of her skin, cool and pale as alabaster: the beauty of her body under the near-transparent muslin.

He gritted his teeth as he looked at the new hand of cards. Unless Foley, Lord Worcester, and Percy Rochester were more unfortunate than he, which seemed unlikely, Brummell would have cause for another admonition in a very short time.

He wasn't sure whether it was pure

bad luck which attended him that night or whether it was because he couldn't concentrate on the game. He would be seeing Bess in two days' time: she wouldn't dare refuse his order to meet him, for all her haughty airs. She had too much to lose, and Bess had never been a fool.

The hand was over, and Barron had lost again. Men were beginning to group themselves near his table, the whisper running round the room that Beau Barron was in over his head, his defeat spectacular.

Greedy eyes watched: bodies pressed together. Many wished him ill, for they had felt the rough side of his tongue, and he was a damned sight too arrogant for their taste. Even the waiters paused, trays balanced, as the atmosphere grew tenser. They had a nose for drama, the ill-paid servants who moved amongst the wealthy and high-born. They could always tell when a streak of good-fortune, or a run of failure, was going to turn from a mere embarrassment to a financial disaster, and to-night was such an occasion.

By five o'clock it was all over. Some

members had drifted away, tired and anxious for their beds, confident that there was no way in which Barron could mend his fortunes. Others hung on, waiting for the kill, tongues moving over dry lips, finishing off a last brandy or a rum.

In defeat, Charles was as unmoved as when he won. He rose from the table, bowing slightly to his opponents.

"Gentlemen, my congratulations. I trust that you will accommodate me for a day or two?"

"Of course." Percy Rochester was triumphant, but although he detested Barron for his supercilious manner, he trusted him implicitly to pay his gambling debts. A tailor's bill might have to wait, but a gentleman never failed to pay losses at the table. "Yes, certainly, sir, for as long as you wish."

"You are a lunatic," said Brummell, as he and Charles left the club.

"You've lost over a hundred thousand, and you haven't got that much."

"Alas no." Charles shrugged. "It'll mean another visit to 'Jew' King in Clarges Street."

"Think he'll help? You've already mortgaged your house and the horses."

Charles smiled faintly.

"My dear George, of course he'll help. That's how he has made his fortune. He'd still be in the gutter where he was born, if he were only prepared to assist those who already had money."

A night watchman passed them by, saluting smartly. These bucks were often good for a coin or two, especially when they'd won, and this time he wasn't disappointed.

"Thank 'e, sir, most kindly. Right generous of you."

"A sovereign? Really, Charles, I sometimes think you are not right in the head."

"It was the last I had. What use is one to me?"

"And if 'Jew' King won't help?"

"Then, m'dear fellow, I'll be bankrupt, won't I?"

The Beau's doubts about 'Jew' King were not unfounded, as Charles soon found out the next day when he arrived at the house in Clarges Street, to which so many in his position had gone before.

"Well, Sir Charles." The 'Jew' was doubtful. "It's a great deal, you know."

"Of course it is." Barron was irritable. "I would hardly have come to you for a few shillings, would I?"

"No, no, but we mustn't forget that your house . . . "

" . . . is already mortgaged. Of course I haven't forgotten." Charles temper was rising. "And the horses, and the carriages. What of it?"

"Not a good risk, you see." The sleek, well-fed moneylender with the hard brown eyes feigned a regretful air. Wouldn't do to offend someone like Sir Charles Barron, yet he wasn't going to throw good money after bad without some thought as to how he would get it back. "What about your wife?"

"My wife?" Barron's brows were threatening. "What the hell do you mean . . . what about my wife?"

King could see the danger, and backed off quickly. These aristocratic young blades could turn nasty very swiftly.

"Nothing, nothing. I just thought that perhaps she . . . "

"Keep your thoughts to yourself,"

snapped Barron. "Now, are you going to lend me the money, you blasted blood-sucker, or aren't you?"

"Have to think about it."

"For Christ's sake!" Barron controlled himself with an effort: No good antagonising the 'Jew' beyond the point of no recall. There wasn't anyone else with a hundred thousand pounds to lend him. "How long are you likely to take to think about so small a matter?"

The 'Jew' smiled unctuously.

"Hardly a little matter, sir, but not long. Say two days."

"No longer." Barron was terse. "Not the grocer's bill, you know. This is a debt of honour."

"Quite so, quite so." The money-lender was opening the door. "Understand perfectly. Two days."

"I told you it wouldn't be easy." Brummell was half-way through his toilet when Barron arrived, Robinson looking as harassed as ever. The breeches had been difficult to get on that morning, and now the Beau was complaining that his shirts, which he always sent to the country to have laundered, because he considered the fresh air better for them, were creased and unwearable. "What are you going to do now?"

Barron was toying with his cane, his mouth a straight line.

"Wait, as I've been told to do. What else can I do?"

"Have an *affaire* with the Duchess of Merton. You know she'd do anything on earth to get you into her bed, and she's so rich she could pay your debts ten times over and never notice it."

"Augusta! God forbid. She's fifty, if she's a day."

"What of it? It's very much the thing for one's mistress to be mature. Look at the prince."

"I'm not the prince, and Augusta FitzCromer is a tyrannical old . . . "

"Yes, but you can't afford to consider that. No, no, you dolt! How can I wear a shirt screwed up like an old rag. Get another, and hurry!"

"Hurry?" Charles looked up from his musings. "You, in a hurry at your toilet? George, what can be the matter with you?"

The Beau gave a secretive smile.

"Never you mind, and don't dismiss Augusta too lightly. If 'Jew' King won't come through, you may have to bow to her discipline. Do you a power of good."

"Bed her yourself, damn you! It might do you even more good."

Barron slammed the door behind him, leaving Brummell chuckling as he turned his attention once more to the selection of a suitable shirt.

* * *

"And they say that he didn't blink an eyelash." Christine Cotter put the finishing touches to Bess's hair, standing back with a sigh. "Oh yes, that is quite splendid."

"Is it known how much Sir Charles lost?" Bess was very casual, picking up a hand mirror to consider the side view of the crisp flick of her curls. "A great deal, I imagine."

"Some say a hundred thousand, some say more." Christine looked unhappy. "Poor man. It's also rumoured that 'Jew' King is unwilling to help him this time.

Nothing to secure the loan, you see."

"Yes, I do indeed see." Bess's lips were smiling, but she wasn't amused. "How very unfortunate for Sir Charles. It seems that he is in a most difficult predicament, wouldn't you say?"

"Oh, the very worst. Is there anything more?"

"No." Bess laid the looking-glass down, no hint of her satisfaction shewing. "I have a letter to write; then you may call the carriage. I am lunching with Lady Foley at one o'clock."

When Christine had gone, Bess sat and gazed at her reflection. She had no letter to write, but she wanted five minutes' peace to consider the new circumstances which Fate had placed so bountifully in her lap. Charles in such debt, and 'Jew' King wouldn't help. And it was a gambling debt too, which had to be paid at all costs. The smile deepened. Yes, indeed; poor Sir Charles was in dire straits.

The next night Bess went to Covent Garden. It hadn't been easy to get away, and she wasn't sure that Thomas had really accepted her headache as an excuse to leave Almack's so early.

She had to bribe the coachman liberally to seal his tongue, dismissing him when she reached her destination, and warning him to return without fail in an hour. Thomas wouldn't leave the club for some while; she would just have time to deal with Barron and be home and in bed before her husband arrived.

She wrinkled her nose in disgust at the smell as she entered the house where once she had been so happy. Everything looked smaller and dirtier than she had remembered, but then, of course, when she had come before she had been in love, and nothing else had mattered.

That night she refused to acknowledge that she was still in love. It would only weaken her resolve, and perhaps rob her of a chance of paying Barron back for the ills he had done her.

He was waiting for her in the room they had always used, and for a second she felt weak. So tall and handsome, his evening-dress immaculate, and ludicrously out of place in such surroundings.

He raised his quizzing-glass and looked her over from head to foot. The gesture was an insult, and she knew that it was meant to be. It took every ounce of her self-possession not to colour up and let him see how much he could still affect her.

"Well, Sir Charles, I'm here. What now?"

"So you are." The drawl was as maddening as the look had been. "As to why you have come, surely there can be no doubt in your mind about that. I told you; you will become my mistress again."

This time she was ready for him.

"Such a signal honour." Her eyes were as mocking as his. "It is a miracle that I do not swoon with ecstasy at the mere thought of it."

Barron's mouth tightened. It was not what he had expected. The threat of exposure should have unnerved Bess and kept her humble. Instead, she was derisive. She was also extremely lovely, and for a second he watched the rise and fall of her breast, her cloak falling back to allow him a glimpse of the tantalizing sight.

"Sarcasm, my dear?" He was still not quite able to accept that this marvellous creature was the child he had almost run down with his curricle. Only a year or two ago, yet such a miraculous change. "I would advise caution. You have much to lose."

He saw the small pearly teeth against the red lips he wanted desperately to kiss, checking himself, because the night would be dictated by his will, not hers.

"Indeed." She let the cloak fall open further. She had chosen a gown which even Thomas had felt somewhat risqué, but she had gazed at him with limpid eyes, assuring him that it was the very latest fashion, and every man would envy him. "You may be right, of course, but in your circumstances you should be sympathetic. After all, you have already lost everything, haven't you?"

Charles let his glass fall, his jaw tightening. So she'd heard. It was hardly surprising, of course, for the whole of London seemed to be aware of his misfortune, and of the 'Jew's' reluctance to help.

"Madam?"

Bess looked at the bed, and then at Barron.

"Sir?"

When he remained silent, she gave a soft laugh.

"Rather a hard mattress, if I recall correctly, but I daresay it will serve, that is, unless you decide to accept the alternative I have to offer."

He was wary, watching her as she laid the cloak on the bed and came towards him. Her perfume was light and expensive, and made him a trifle giddy. Her body, so close to his, was a deliberate provocation. She was taunting him, making him sweat unseen, and yet she knew what he could do to her reputation. It made him uneasy.

"Alternative? What have you in mind?"

He wasn't going to let Bess see what she could do to him by her nearness. She needed a good lesson, and in a very short time he intended to give her one.

"Well . . . " A small pink tongue moistened the inviting lips; the curve of her half-clad bosom was used as a weapon. "We could make love, of course. You could force me to that, for, as you say, you could expose me. But what is a romp amongst the sheets, and filthy ones at that, compared with a settlement of your debts, and more besides."

He frowned.

"Settlement of my debts? What are you talking about?"

"Oh come, do you imagine that I haven't heard how foolish you've been? One hundred thousand, wasn't it, and the 'Jew' not ready to come to your aid."

"He will. He's thinking it over."

"He will refuse."

His frown was deeper; a threat to her.

"How do you know? Have you been meddling? If so . . . "

"Not meddling." She smiled sweetly. "Just making sure that the plan I have will be accepted by you. To that end I paid the 'Jew' to keep his money. He won't help you, but I will."

Her amusement died as suddenly as it had come.

"Me, Charles, or one hundred and fifty thousand pounds."

After a deadly silence lasting some sixty seconds, Barron said coldly:

"You put a high price on yourself, my girl."

"I am not your girl, and never will be again."

"How can you raise such a sum?"

She gave a taunting laugh, which made him want to hit her.

"Very easily, I assure you. I gamble too, but with much better results. I always know when to stop, you see. Besides, the three brothels which I own are so profitable I scarcely know what to do with the income they bring in. Naturally, Thomas doesn't know about them; no one in our circle does, except you. And you won't mention them, my dear, because it is from them that the money is coming to save your skin."

This time the silence was longer. Then Barron said very quietly:

"You hate me that much? You would pay so much to avoid sleeping with me? Yes, I suppose you would. You said you'd make me crawl, didn't you?"

"I did." She was quite calm, not letting him see either her satisfaction, or the other feeling which was growing stronger the closer she was to him. "And crawling you are. You can't afford the luxury of humiliating me, can you? You need the money far too much. It'll be with you to-morrow morning, and not a soul shall be any the wiser as to where it came from. Even sluts like me understand honour, you know."

"It is a costly revenge." He was sombre. "Is it really worth it?"

"Every penny, and more. You'll never take me again, Charles Barron."

They glared at each other. She was disappointed that he had shewn no sign of being humbled. His face was as impassive as ever, and she was furious. But under the anger, she wanted him. She wanted him to tell her to keep her money, and throw her across the bed, tearing her dress off, so that she could feel the touch of his hands on her.

For his part, Charles was as livid as Bess. She had worsted him, twisting his victory into her triumph, and he would like to have beaten her soundly for her insolence. For a second he was tempted to reject the offer and take her there and then, but he knew that he could not afford to. He would have to swallow both rage and pride, and whatever strange feeling it was that she aroused in him, and admit defeat, and it galled him.

"Very well," he said stiffly, "I accept your terms. Your money, ill-gotten though it be, for my silence."

"A bargain." She was brittle, her face harder than marble. "And don't be so contemptuous of the source of your salvation. Some of the money is yours, no doubt; yours, and your companions, who visit the *bagnios* and use the girls as if they were slaves, born simply to afford you pleasure."

He said nothing, but she couldn't stop her goading. She wanted him to shew his injury so that she could gloat over it. His acceptance of her terms, without a flicker of expression, wasn't enough.

"And just to shew you what you have missed by agreeing to my proposal, look well, sir, and decide if you've made a good bargain."

Before he could move she had stripped the gown off and was standing naked before him, eyes bright with unshed tears, her mouth unsteady.

He thought he had never seen so wonderful a sight in all his life, hardly able to believe that this was the same girl he had taken so casually in that very room. But, of course, it wasn't the same girl. Bess had changed, and not only in looks. He said softly:

"Oh yes, you do hate me. Get dressed; don't do this to yourself, it isn't necessary. You have brought me low; that's enough."

When she had pulled her clothes on and fastened the cloak, her tears were over. Her gesture had gone wrong too. His reaction had not been what she had expected, and she felt ashamed, unclean, and petty.

She was trying to think of a stinging remark to make upon her exit, when Charles said:

"The child?"

She gave a short laugh.

"Dead, but how clever of you to remember. Your sovereigns weren't enough; I had to work twenty hours a day, and that killed my baby."

"I'm sorry," he said after a second or two. "Bess, I'm truly sorry."

"Elizabeth, and I am not in the least sorry. I'm glad it didn't live. I want nothing left to remind me of you. You shall have your money in the morning."

Outside, she could feel her legs shaking so much that she wondered if she would ever get down the stairs without tumbling head first. She didn't care that she was crying now, for no one could see her deep misery.

What on earth had possessed her to cheapen herself in front of Charles in that brazen manner? She thought she had left such behaviour far behind her, but it seemed that even Thomas's exalted name hadn't erased all of the old Bess Hathaway.

Slowly she descended the last flight, almost blinded by her grief. The evening had been hers, but it was a hollow victory. She loved Charles as much as ever, and if he had but known how she longed for him to take her in his arms it would have been she who suffered defeat, and of the worst kind.

But he didn't know, and never would. She wiped the tears away, holding the cloak tightly round her as if she didn't want anyone in the world to see her body, ever again.

"Home, m'lady?"

"Yes, Shepherd, and please hurry." She turned to look up at the house, seeing only the darkness, but knowing Charles was still there. "Yes, as quickly as you can, for there is nothing left here for me now."

5

THREE months later, there was a splendid ball at Almack's. Every ball at that most exclusive club tended to be splendid, but this one seemed to outdo all its predecessors.

Bess and Thomas arrived late, but were soon swept up in the music and excitement, wine flowing, and gossip as spiteful and damaging as ever.

Bess had been determined to forget that night with Charles, trying to put the whole sorry episode out of her mind, but it hadn't been possible. She couldn't forget him, or her own behaviour, blaming him the more because he still had so much power over her.

She had kept her word, and his debts had been paid. Many whispers circulated about the source of Barron's sudden wealth, and 'Jew' King, who had not been called upon to assist on this occasion, merely cackled, and waited for Charles to lose again.

Bess wished she could get rid of the brothels. Suddenly, her ownership of them was beginning to worry her. Charles would never speak of them, of that she was sure, but it would be all too easy for someone else to find out, and then she would be ruined.

She was tempted on many occasions to sell, but the sale itself would be risky. Besides, they produced the most rewarding of dividends, and Thomas, for all his wealth, tended to be parsimonious. In the first few weeks of marriage he had showered gifts upon her, begrudging her nothing, but when the initial magic had worn off his true nature had taken over again, and he exclaimed in vexation at the size of her bills, declaring that her hats must be made of spun gold to cost so much.

Soon, she began to pay many of the accounts herself, producing just enough for Thomas to foot so that he did not become suspicious. She was tiring of Thomas too, for he was a feeble lover, and his increasing girth was a poor exchange for Charles's broad shoulders and lean flanks.

Once or twice she had even considered running away, but such absurd notions were soon put aside. Where could she run to, and why should she forgo her social position? She would have to put up with Thomas's crude grapplings in order that she could continue to snub Sir Charles Barron and his dowdy wife.

She was dancing with the prince, who was again honouring Almack's that night with his presence, talking of music, of which he was vastly fond, and very knowledgeable.

"Look quite remarkable to-night, m'dear," he said when the music stopped, and a waiter hurried up with champagne. "Yes, quite remarkable."

She smiled demurely, not averse to a mild flirtation with the king's son, for he really was the most amiable of men, and she had grown quite fond of him.

"Thank you, sir, but I swear that you bring a blush to my cheeks with such flattery."

"No flattery, but the blush is mighty becomin'. Said it before; will say it again. Thomas is damned lucky."

She knew that he was about to bend

to kiss her cheek, wondering whether to draw back slightly and risk offending him, or whether to allow the caress, trusting that the Gorgons gathered together in front of the fireplace wouldn't notice.

It was then that she became aware of a disturbance; of voices raised, and a woman screaming.

"Eh? What?" The prince straightened up at once, annoyed that he hadn't been able to feel the smoothness of the countess's cheek against his lips. Lovely filly; he'd have to see what could be done to get closer to her. "What's all the fuss about, Alvanley?"

Alvanley had come hurrying up, face like whey, his hands outstretched to Bess.

"Got to be brave, dear lady," he said, his voice ragged. "All over in a minute. Wouldn't have known a thing about it."

"Who wouldn't have known a thing about what?" The prince was testy. "What on earth are you talking about, and why are you holding the countess's hands like that? Impudence, if you ask me."

"Sir, it's Thomas. Heart attack, don't you know. Gone in an instant."

Bess was stunned, hardly aware of the prince's sudden and genuine concern as he and Alvanley led her to where Thomas lay still and silent. The revellers had drawn back, clearing a space round the body, some scared, some awed, even some put out by the bad taste shewn by the earl in meeting his Maker in the middle of a ball at Almack's.

Everyone was very kind to Bess, and she went through the pretence of grieving for Thomas for a whole month. Then she emerged, an extremely rich woman, for Thomas had left her everything. She had managed to rid herself of the brothels; she didn't need their profits now, and they were even more of a danger than before.

She spent money like water, on clothes, jewels, horses, carriages, and cards, consistently lucky at faro and macao, thus adding to her already enormous fortune.

She flirted with many, including the prince, but caring for none, and keeping every man at arm's length. Since she didn't want any man but Charles, the exercise caused her no problem, and she found that it enhanced her attraction and made her suitors more ardent.

She still met Charles and Adelaide, but neither she nor Barron ever shewed that they were more than acquaintances. Only once, when she found herself dancing with Charles, did their eyes meet, and the effect of that was sufficient to cause her to beg his forgiveness, and hurry off the floor.

She was wondering how long her life would remain so empty when one night she attended a fancy-dress ball given by Lady Foley. She didn't particularly want to go, but the alternative was the card-tables at Almack's, or a lonely evening in her new house in Grosvenor Square, considering the priceless pictures and ornaments which bedecked it.

Perversely, she had decided against the costume of an Eastern princess which Christine wanted her to wear.

"No, no," she had said crossly, "I don't like it, and every other woman will have the same idea."

"But it is so charming." Miss

Cotter's nose had been quivering with disappointment, tears not far off. "See how I have sewn the pearls and spangles on the skirt; so rich."

"So gaudy, and the neck's too low."

"Not lower than . . . "

"Hold your tongue! I'm not going to wear it, and if you are daring to say that I wear gowns as indiscreet as the Princess Caroline, you might care to remember . . . oh, Christine!"

Bess had been remorseful, holding the small body against her own.

"Love, I'm a shrew, and I don't mean a word of it."

"I know." Christine had sniffed and fumbled for her handkerchief. "It's quite all right; really it is."

"No, it isn't. I'm as vindictive as those harpies at Almack's, and an ungrateful wretch to treat you so when you have done so much for me. Oh, why don't you put on some weight! You're like a starving sparrow."

"Well, it's not through trying on your part, for I declare I am so well fed here that by rights I should be the size of a barrel." Miss Cotter had been herself again. "I'm an old silly to press you to do something you don't want to do. What costume will you choose instead?"

Bess had given a small, controlled smile.

"I shall go as a beggar-girl; that'll turn a few heads. Make me a skirt, and a loose blouse, and cut the neck as low as you like; I don't care a button."

And she didn't. The patronesses of Almack's, all guests of Lady Foley, looked askance at the skimpiness of the skirt and the quite disgraceful line of the neck of Bess's costume.

"Do you care for my disguise, Lady Jersey?" asked Bess, head high, daring the lady in question to put her down. "So original, don't you think? I was advised to adopt the costume of an Eastern princess, but I thought it far too ordinary, do you not agree?"

The response was a frosty silence, and Bess smiled brightly.

"Oh dear! I fear that I have been mightily tactless, for I do declare that you are wearing such a guise yourself. So stupid of me."

She moved off, leaving Lady Jersey red

with indignation, and soundly denouncing the countess as an ill-mannered upstart, a view which Lady Castlereagh and Mrs Drummond-Burrell heartily endorsed.

It was half-way through the evening before Charles arrived, making his excuses, and explaining that Adelaide was in bed with a cold.

"Your wife seems to suffer a good deal from colds, Sir Charles," remarked Lady Castlereagh coldly. "One might almost think that you were trying to hide her away."

"Nothing was further from my thoughts." Barron bowed over her hand. "She shall attend the very next function, I promise you."

He moved on, leaving tongues wagging faster than ever, meeting Bess alone by the window where she was seeking a moment's quietness and a breath of fresh air.

"Your servant." He kissed her finger-tips, as if they had only just met. "Alone? A most unusual state of affairs."

The hard eyes were calculating as they ran over her costume.

"Reverting to type, are you, Bess?"

"Elizabeth," she said through grinding teeth. "And please go away. I want to be alone. If I didn't, I could have any man I wanted by my side."

"Your conceit is only superseded by your boldness in wearing that thing. Why did you bother to put the blouse on? It does little to cover that with which Nature has endowed you."

"Go away! If you don't, I swear I shall call for help."

"You wouldn't do that, my dear." He was smooth, keeping her hand in his. "It would only convince the whole company here that you were a hussy, which, of course, you are. Waiter, more wine."

"I don't want any wine."

"Drink it, and be quiet."

"I won't . . . I . . . oh!"

The grip of his fingers tightened, and she gave a gasp.

"Charles! You're hurting me."

"Then be silent and drink your wine." He was surveying the room with distaste. "God, why do I come to these dull and pointless parties?"

"I have no idea. Why don't you stay home with your wife? I'm sure that she would be grateful for a little of your attention."

He considered her thoughtfully.

"A somewhat feline remark. Don't you like Adelaide? No, of course, I remember now; you don't. I seem to recall that I had to rebuke you once for your rudeness to her."

"How like you to remind me of that." Her eyes sparkled with vexation. "Do go away! I cannot bear to listen to you any longer."

"How strange, for I quite enjoy listening to you; it reminds me of old times."

"You mean I sound like Bess from Southwark?" Her cheeks were growing warmer. "You'll never let me forget that, will you?"

"It is you who remind me, first with your extraordinary manners, and now with that costume. Drink up, and have another. What else is there to do?"

Two hours later, Charles and Bess were more than tipsy. They hadn't rejoined the dancers, but had wandered out into an ante-room, where there was plenty of food and drink.

"I think I should take you home," said Barron at last. "I swear this is the fourth time you have fallen off that chair."

She giggled and tried to get up.

"Fiff . . . fiff . . . fifth. I want another drink."

"When you get home; not here."

"I want it . . . want it now."

"Well, you're not going to have it." He hauled her to her feet, laughing with her, as her knees buckled, lifting her up in his arms.

"Not as heavy as you were, you saucy mermaid."

"Mer . . . mermaid's a whore."

"And so are you. Now hush; my phaeton's over here."

Somehow he got her on to the seat, and took the reins in his hands. He felt wildly excited, as if Lady Foley's champagne had had some special ingredient in it which had made *ennui*, and dissatisfaction with life, fade away.

"Tell your servants to go to bed," he whispered as they crossed the hall to the stairs. "Get rid of them."

Bess started to laugh, ignoring her butler's pained expression.

"Go . . . go . . . away, Bateman." She managed to get the words out at last. "Go to bed; all of you . . . go . . . go to bed."

"But your guest, m'lady?"

"I'll see to him." She sank down on the stairs, giggling again. "Off you go . . . I'll see to him."

They waited as the butler withdrew in disgust; then they started to laugh again.

"He thinks I'm a mer . . . mermaid too," she whispered. "Oh dear, I'm afraid I'm drunk, Charles. You'll have to carry me up to my room."

"I'm afraid I'm drunk too, but no doubt we'll manage. After all, I managed well enough when you were as fat as a pudding."

"I was never fat! Just nicely rounded."

"Fat as a sow."

"Don't be horrid, not to-night. Whoops! You've dropped me!"

"So I have."

They clung together, helpless with mirth, until finally Barron managed to drag Bess to her feet and hoisted her up, not listening to her protests.

"Which room, my fair Cyprian? In which bed does my delicious warming-pan lie at nights?"

"Warming-pan's a whore too." She bit his ear. "Don't call me a trollop, Charles Barron, or I'll bite you again."

"Do so, by all means, if you don't mind being bitten in return. This one? Praise be to God! You may look like a feather, my girl, but one should be more sober than I am at the moment to drag you about over one's shoulder."

They collapsed on the bed, still chuckling, until suddenly all the amusement was gone, and Charles was holding her tightly against him, his mouth no more than an inch from hers.

"No!" Just as suddenly, Bess threw off the effects of the drink, trying frantically to pull away from him. "No, Charles, you shan't! You shan't! I won't have it; I won't!"

He didn't answer, one hand slowly pulling the blouse from her shoulders.

"No! No! It isn't fair! I paid your debts; you're cheating me. Leave me alone . . . oh, Charles! Don't! Don't!"

She felt her flesh against his own, his

arms hard round her. When he kissed her, she clung to him as if she would never let him go. All her protests and indignation vanished; she was simply conscious that she was with the man she loved, and that his hand was moving seductively along her thigh until she could have screamed with the aching longing inside herself.

Then all pretence was done, and they came together in rabid hunger and desire. Bess moaned, her eyes closed, her body fused with his until the dreadful emptiness of life without him had gone. She didn't want him to release her, but in the end he sat up and smiled.

"You're a fool, Bess. We should have done that a long time ago."

"Maybe." She lay back, contented and happier than she had been for months. "You were always a good lover, even if you can't win a simple game of cards."

"Be quiet, you slut." He wasn't angry. On the contrary, he too was filled with a quiet, deep peace. "This can't be the last time; you know that. We must meet again."

"Where?" She didn't deny him. He

was right; they had to meet again. "Not here. There would be too much talk."

"The house in Covent Garden was always convenient, and who would think of looking for the Countess of Crayford there?"

"Or even Sir Charles Barron."

Bess wasn't offended this time by his suggestion. She didn't care where they met, so long as she could have him.

"All right. When? To-morrow?"

"Greedy."

"The next day then?"

And the next day it was, and two or three times a week thereafter. Bess was careful, always making plausible excuses to her household. She didn't know whether they believed her: it wasn't important. It was none of their business, and she needed Charles like the air she breathed. She thought Christine and her maid looked at her oddly when she sang whilst they dressed her; that Bateman regarded her suspiciously when she almost danced downstairs, but she ignored them all. Let them think what they would: say what they would. Charles was hers again, and that was all that counted.

"What would Adelaide say if she could see us now?" she asked the next time they lay together on the hard bed. "Would she care?"

Barron didn't turn his head, schooling his face to immobility.

"I doubt it. She knows I'm not faithful, and she's not a hot polecat, like you."

"But if she knew it wasn't just a casual thing." Bess curled up beside him, stroking his arm. "What if she knew that we were in love? What then?"

"You ask too many questions." He said it lightly, looking down at her. "We haven't come here to talk about Adelaide."

"What have we come for?" She teased him. "I thought it was to make love, not talk."

"It's you who is doing all the talking." He slapped her bottom, laughing reluctantly. "You really are a badger, Bess, d'you know that? I've never met a woman who enjoyed bed as much as you do."

She smiled blissfully.

"I'm glad. I wouldn't want any rivals. Oh, Charles, I really do adore you."

He held her away a moment longer, almost frowning at her intensity. Then he gave a faint sigh and pulled her closer, covering her eager lips with his own.

* * *

Adelaide's maid shook her head.

"Madam, I really think you ought to tell the master. He's got to know sooner or later, hasn't he?"

Adelaide's hands fluttered helplessly.

"No, Morna, no. I cannot tell him."

"But why not? M'm, he'd be so pleased to know that . . ."

"No he wouldn't." Adelaide's lips were pressed together in a stubborn line. Like many shy and pliant people, there were occasions on which she could be very pig-headed, and this was one of them. "No, I don't think he would be interested, for he doesn't care for me at all, you see."

"Now, how can you say such a thing?" Morna Hicks was a motherly woman who had taken the place of the girl Adelaide had brought with her from Austria, and who had proved too susceptible to Charles's male staff. "Every man wants a son."

"It could be a girl, and look like me, and then he'd dislike it, just as he dislikes me."

"What nonsense! A pretty lady like you."

"Pretty!" Adelaide stared at Morna in astonishment. "You think that I'm pretty?"

"Of course I do." The maid brushed out the dark, wiry hair, the movements slow and soothing. "So does master, I'll be bound."

Adelaide got up and went to the bed, allowing Morna to hold back the sheets and then smooth the coverlet. She longed to tell the woman with the round, rosy face and sunny smile that she knew Charles was unfaithful, but she couldn't do it. She was aware that many women talked without reserve to their maids, but that was not in her nature. The matter was one between Charles and herself, no matter how much she longed for Morna's sympathy.

She had known of Charles's reputation almost since their marriage, but it hadn't troubled her unduly. Men, her mother had told her firmly, had to have their own way in such things. A wife's place was to endure with fortitude such lapses and never to shew an awareness of mistresses, many of whom, her mother had continued, were no better than common prostitutes.

But one day, when she and Charles had been dining with the Alvanleys, Adelaide had happened to glance up, just in time to catch a look exchanged between the Countess of Crayford and Charles. It was a fleeting thing, and the lovely woman with the red-gold hair had been as aloof and contemptuous as ever, yet in that single second Adelaide had read the truth.

She thought perhaps the certainty came from her own love of Charles. Everything about him was important to her: since that night when he had made love to her, and taken all the fear away, he had been her whole world. Whilst everyone else remarked on the coolness between Sir Charles Barron and Elizabeth Merchant, Adelaide, at least, had known the truth.

It was useless to stay awake for Charles,

for he seldom got home until the early hours of the morning, and even when he did arrive more often than not he used his dressing-room.

But sleep wouldn't come, and Adelaide sat up and hugged her knees. Perhaps she was wrong after all. No one else seemed to have an inkling of what she suspected, and since the patronesses of Almack's knew everything about everyone, surely some hint of the *affaire* between Charles and Elizabeth would have leaked out if it had been true.

"Still awake, my dear?"

Adelaide started. She had been so engrossed in her dark thoughts that she hadn't heard the door open.

"Oh . . . Charles . . . you startled me."

"I'm sorry." He came over to the bed. "Why are you still awake? It's very late."

"I know." She turned her head away, not wanting him to probe further. "Please do not concern yourself about me."

"Why shouldn't I? You're my wife."

At that, she did look at him, and he grimaced. There was no mistaking the accusation in her eyes. He grew very still, wondering if she knew about Bess, and, if so, who had told her. It was important that he found out, and was blunt about it.

"You seem displeased with me. Do you suspect me of dallying with some woman? If so, you're wrong. I've been playing cards with Brummell."

"To-night, maybe."

Her voice was colder and more confident than he had ever heard it; as if she had suddenly grown from a self-conscious girl to a mature woman.

"What does that mean?"

"What should it mean, sir? You know better than any how you spend your nights. Certainly few enough are spent in my bed."

He leaned over and took her face between his hands.

"Adelaide? Who's been talking to you?"

"No one." She didn't move, although his touch was making her pulse quicken. "No one has spoken to me; it wasn't necessary."

"Very well." His hands dropped, and

he was as curt as she. "I have sought company elsewhere from time to time: it is not important."

"It is to me, for it means that I don't satisfy you, and that makes me sad. Was she beautiful?"

"Who?"

"The woman you love."

It was a moment of truth for both of them, and they knew it. Charles chose to lie, and Adelaide withdrew from the contest, because, at the last moment, she really didn't want to know the answer.

"There is no particular woman. Just a demi-rep or two, who appealed to me when I was in my cups."

"I see."

The deceipt was accepted passively, and Charles breathed again. She didn't know about Elizabeth. She was just angry because he hadn't paid sufficient attention to her, a fault he tried to put right without delay.

"Shall I stay with you to-night?"

Her eyes moved to his again.

"No thank you."

"Don't be childish. Such things mean nothing."

"I know that."

"Then . . . "

"I don't want you."

"You are my wife. What if I want you?"

"You don't." She couldn't help the tears spilling over, her frail body hunched up in unhappiness. "You've never wanted me. Even when you lost so much money, you went to that Jew. You could have come to me. I have jewellery worth a fortune. I would have sold it all to help you. Even then, you didn't want me. You shut me out: I was no use to you."

"How did you hear about that? The debts, I mean?" He was harsh, gripping her arms until she whimpered. "Who told you?"

"I . . . I . . . can't remember. It doesn't matter, does it? The Jew lent you the money, and since then you have won, so I hear."

"You hear a great deal too much, madam." She was released abruptly. "And I would never ask you to sell your possessions for me."

"But I would have done so gladly. Don't you understand? I would have done anything . . . I would still do anything to . . . "

Her voice became muffled as she buried her face in her hands, and his anger drained away.

"Don't, Adelaide, don't." He caught her, and let her cry against his shoulder. "Enough, sweet, enough."

He wondered why the feel of her meant so little to him; why Bess could make him feel like a god, whilst his own wife could arouse no more in him than pity.

"I . . . I . . . think I'd like you to stay after all," said Adelaide with a watery smile. "Not to . . . well . . . that is . . . I just want you to be near to me."

He nodded, grateful that he wouldn't have to assume a passion he didn't feel, lying down beside her and stroking her hair. It was almost rough against his hand, not like Bess's, which was pure silk with sunlight in it.

She was asleep in no time, but he lay awake until morning. His marriage was a farce, and Elizabeth was free. He tried to dislike Adelaide, for her very existence, which kept him apart from Bess, but he couldn't. How could one dislike a harmless, pathetic being like Adelaide?

The patronesses of Almack's were not so forbearing as he, and when next Adelaide visited the club, Mrs Drummond-Burrell skilfully detached the unfortunate girl, leaving Barron to discuss the latest style of top coat with George Brummell.

"We would not normally interfere," said that august lady with more conviction than truth, "but you are a mere child, and have no mother to advise you."

Adelaide was still in terror of the patronesses, but she tried not to shew it.

"I don't understand," she whispered. "What have I done?"

"Nothing, my dear, nothing," replied Lady Cowper quickly. "Don't look like that; we're not really as fierce as some say we are."

"It is not our reputation which is at stake," said Lady Castlereagh repressively. "It is, I fear, your husband's, Lady Barron."

"But . . . "

"Now, I beg you not to argue, but to listen, for we know a great deal more about the world than you do. We also know far more about Charles than you appear to."

"But . . . "

"You do not stand up to him." Countess Lieven was pure scorn. The girl was like a frightened rabbit. It really didn't seem worth while trying to help her, but the others had been insistent. "Your husband gambles too much, drinks too much, and rides those horses of his so fast that no one can understand why he hasn't broken his neck before this. It is true, of course, that good horsemanship is an essential quality for any gentleman of breeding, but the way he races those brutes is quite another thing."

"Furthermore," Lady Jersey was sharp, "there is no doubt that he visits some quite deplorable places at night, and shews no discretion at all in doing so. You must put your foot down."

Adelaide could feel the room swaying about her. She knew that what the patronesses were saying was true, and, in a way, their strictures on Charles's visits to the brothels was a relief. It confirmed his own assurance that there was no one woman for whom he cared, but simply that he sought something which she couldn't give him.

"Quick!" Lady Cowper moved hastily to catch the fainting Adelaide. "Let us get her out of here. No fuss; bring her through to the ante-room where there's more air. Why, the poor thing looks like a ghost."

When Adelaide recovered she found she had not lost her inquisitors. They encircled her, hovering like birds of prey, and she wanted to scream at them to go away and stop tormenting her.

"*Ma pauvre petite!*" Princess Esterhazy dimpled, and patted Adelaide's hand. "Why did you not tell us that you were enceinte? We would not have plagued you so."

"We were not plaguing Lady Barron." Mrs Drummond-Burrell was severe. "It was for her own good, but now that we know she is with child, perhaps our assistance will not be necessary. Maybe this will bring Charles to a proper sense of how he should behave."

"Was he pleased when you told him?" The kindly Lady Sefton was holding

Adelaide's hand. "Oh, but I'm sure he must have been."

"I . . . I . . . haven't told him."

"What!" Mrs Drummond-Burrell was horrified. "You are carrying his child, and you haven't told him? What can you be thinking about? You must tell him at once."

"But . . . he will be so angry."

Mrs Drummond-Burrell was almost silenced for once, but not quite.

"Angry, because you are going to have a child? What utter nonsense, particularly as he is responsible."

A stillness fell. The ladies exchanged looks, charged with doubt. Then Lady Cowper said gently:

"How terrible you must think us, my dear, but are you saying the baby is not your husband's?"

Adelaide began to cry, and Lady Sefton put an arm round her and held her close.

"There, there, my love, don't upset yourself so. You must tell us who the man is, and . . . "

Adelaide pulled herself free and stood up, flushed and, for once, more than a match for the ogres she usually dreaded.

"The child is my husband's, and I shall tell him about it in my own good time. When I said I thought he would be angry I simply meant that he has said in the past that I am too young."

"Rubbish!"

Adelaide glared at Mrs Drummond-Burrell.

"Yes, as you say, rubbish, for I have proved that I am plenty old enough. But it is no business of yours. I hate England, and I hate you all, for you are wretched busybodies with spite in your hearts and poison on your tongues. I hope that I never have to see any of you again."

"Well, really!" Mrs Drummond-Burrell stared at the door which had banged behind Adelaide, "Never have I known such base ingratitude. We do our best to help, and . . . "

Princess Esterhazy opened her fan, moving it gracefully back and forth.

"She may be right, you know."

Lady Jersey was shocked, and said so.

"No, no." The princess smiled, and held up a hand. "I was not agreeing with her most unkind assessment of our blameless characters."

Lady Jersey didn't like the twinkle in the princess's blue eyes. There were times when she thought this young woman a good deal too flippant.

"Then what were you talking about, pray?"

"Charles Barron's reaction when he hears that he is to become a papa." The fan flipped back and forth again. "I believe there is something different about him these days. You are right in all that you say about him, but just lately there has been . . . oh . . . how can I explain?"

"I really don't know." Lady Jersey was short. "He seems the same to me."

"No." Lady Cowper was thoughtful. "I think the princess is right. There is a difference. He looks happier; not so cold. When he thinks no one is watching, he almost smiles with tenderness."

"Good gracious! You talk as if you thought he were . . . in love."

Lady Jersey finished the sentence abruptly, and a delicious shiver went through the group.

"Yes, of course!" Princess Esterhazy

clapped her hands, the fan forgotten. "Yes, and I should have recognised it at once. Charles Barron is in love for the first time in his life. Now, my dears, only one question remains. Who is the woman he loves?"

"There is another question." Mrs Drummond-Burrell was smugly satisfied. "What is she going to say when she hears that his wife is going to bear him a child?"

6

"ARE you pleased, sir?" Adelaide's dark eyes were fixed anxiously on Charles. She didn't like the way he stood so still, nor the rigid line of his mouth. "You are not angry?"

"No, of course not." He said it mechanically, scarcely looking at her. "I am delighted. You must take care of yourself."

"And the child."

"Naturally; and the child."

"I am sorry that I was so foolish the other night. I had no right to tax you with such things." Adelaide had a new softness about her; a kind of inner glow, which made her seem almost pretty. "Now things will be different, won't they? When you have a son you will not want to go to such places as those . . . "

"I fear that you know little of the world." Charles was drawing on his gloves, still stunned by Adelaide's announcement. "But, yes, things may be different."

"Aren't you going to kiss me before you go?" Adelaide held out her hands. "We must grow closer, my dear, before our infant comes."

He barely touched her forehead, leaving her quickly before he betrayed himself.

It was a shattering blow, and one which he hadn't expected. True, he had lain with his wife a sufficient number of times, more from convention than desire, but the notion of the natural consequences of his actions had never occurred to him.

He cursed aloud as he got into his carriage. His life was becoming so complicated that he scarcely knew where to turn for a moment's peace. Adelaide, clinging, helpless, and now with child: Bess, desirable, warm, and the pivot of his existence, although he had never told her so, lest she gained the upper hand. He continued to treat her with the casual indifference of their first meeting, although many times he wanted to drop the mask and tell her how much he cared. And what would Bess make of Adelaide's news? She would probably know already, for Adelaide had spared him no detail of her interrogation by the patronesses. If they knew, the whole world would know too, including Bess.

He had chosen a four-in-hand that morning, trotting briskly out of London and into the open country, where he could think things out. His technique was superb, his hands gentle but firm on the reins. He knew exactly what each of the bays was about, able to urge a slack wheeler, or discourage an over-eager one without the other horses being aware of it. Even at night, Barron's judgment was faultless, knowing just when to let the animals have their heads, and when to check them, assessing to the split second the speed they were doing.

Although he raced so fast that day, there was nothing careless about his driving. Even on the most treacherous of bends he coaxed the wheelers to follow the leading horses in a smooth semicircle, the latter having been pointed carefully into the turn.

When he returned and handed the

sweating bays to his grooms, he divested himself of the dusty coat and pantaloons, dressing again with a speed which made Pengelly moan.

"Sir, the coat is not set right, and the boots . . . "

"Damnation to them both." Barron picked up a duelling-pistol, an inheritance from his father. "Here, put this on your head, and let me see if my eye has lost its cunning."

Pengelly sighed in resignation. It was not that he was afraid of his master missing: Barron never missed. It was simply that his own reputation was at stake, and if Sir Charles walked into White's with a crease like that across the shoulders he would never be able to hold his head up again. Robinson was already a sight too pleased with himself, being in charge of the great Brummell; when they next met over a pot of ale Robinson would have plenty to say about a valet who couldn't attend his master better than that.

There was a sharp crack, and the china ornament splintered to the floor.

"I'm off." Barron put the gun away.

"Tell Lady Barron I shall be late tonight."

"Yes, sir, but your coat!"

"To hell with my coat."

"Yes, sir, to hell with your coat."

Pengelly's sigh came from the bottom of his boots, as sadly he began to pick up the pieces of the Dresden shepherdess.

* * *

It was only a matter of time before Bess heard of Adelaide's condition. She felt as though someone had punched her hard in the stomach, but she had learned her lessons well, and no trace of her agony shewed on her face.

"Really? Yes, Christine, a touch more rouge, I think."

Her personal maid was ill, and Christine was delighted to be helping Bess to dress again. It had hurt a bit when the Frenchwoman had arrived, but she had been philosophical. After all, she hadn't had the training of Charmaine, and the Countess of Crayford must have the best.

"Yes, it's said that Sir Charles is delighted."

"No doubt he is." The voice was toneless, but inside Bess was screaming. "Now the perfume."

In the coach, she lay back, feeling sick. It was absurd of her to imagine for a moment that Charles wasn't sleeping with his wife, yet the thought of a child had never crossed her mind. She, Bess, was Charles's mistress, but the plain, scrawny Adelaide was his wife, and would be the mother of his son. For a second, Bess wondered what her own stillborn child had been. She would never let the midwife tell her, putting her hands over her ears when the woman had tried to speak. She hadn't wanted the dead scrap of humanity to be real, but now she wondered.

By the time the evening was over Bess had drunk too much, and her pain had been turned to raw spite by brandy and wine. Charles should have told her. He shouldn't have let her find out from Christine. It was inexcusable, and heartless, and so like Charles.

Bess found Miss Cotter, dozing in a chair, waiting for her.

"Go to bed," said Bess, not letting

the older woman see the rage which was running right through her, down to her finger-tips. "But before you go, tell Bateman I want to despatch a note to someone: tell him to send one of the boys to me."

"To-night?"

The green eyes were so hard that Christine drew back. She knew that Bess had been drinking heavily: she could smell it on her breath, see the unsteady gait.

"Certainly, to-night. Do as I say, please."

She waited until Christine had hurried from the room, then she went to her writing-desk. She had no idea whether Adelaide was aware that she, Bess, was Charles's mistress. Probably not. The girl was so dense it wouldn't have occurred to her that Charles was unfaithful at all, but she would learn. The quill wavered, and her mind began to blur as she started to write.

The graphic description of one night with Charles in the seedy room at Covent Garden made ugly reading, but Bess was hardly aware of the words she had used.

She simply sealed the note with grim satisfaction, and sent the boy off with it to Charles's residence.

"Don't let a servant have it." Bess was sharp, coming out of her alcoholic haze long enough to give her last instruction. "See that you give it to Lady Barron yourself, do you understand?"

The boy was received somewhat doubtfully, but in the end his earnest explanation of his mistress's insistence that he hand the letter personally to Lady Barron was accepted.

Adelaide was about to retire, but she had a smile for the lad, and a small gold coin to give, which made his face light up in disbelief.

She read the letter, uncomprehendingly at first. She had never seen such things written down before; indeed, she had never heard of such things being done. Every tiny detail of Charles's love-making with the Countess of Crayford was set out so explicitly that Adelaide began to tremble. No wonder Charles had found her so dull and tame; who wouldn't, with a mistress like Elizabeth Merchant?

The savage malice of the note didn't

strike Adelaide at all; she was too stunned by Charles's lie. Not just a Cyprian now and then, but a deep, enduring relationship, which was obviously of long standing.

Adelaide sat for a long while by her bed, simply staring down at the note in her hand. She didn't have to read the message again, for every word of it was seared into her brain.

When her maid came with hot milk, she quickly slid the paper under her pillow, quite composed as she got between the sheets and started to sip her drink.

"Now, you're to finish every drop." Morna Hicks was busy tucking the coverlet into place. "Good for the bairn, and you too."

In the candle-light she paused to scan her mistress's face.

"Look a bit peaky, you do. Are you feeling sick again?"

"No." It was a lie, for Adelaide wanted to retch, not because of the seed in her womb, but because of the horrifying revelations of Elizabeth Merchant. "No, Morna, I'm just tired. I shall be quite myself in the morning, you'll see."

"I hope so. Well, sleep well, and God bless."

The few words of comfort made Adelaide shiver again. A pittance of kindness, and a wealth of cruelty. She wanted to cry, but the tears wouldn't come. All she could do was to lean back against the pillows and think of Charles and the woman who could rouse him, as she, Adelaide, could never do.

At last, when she was certain that the servants had retired, Adelaide flung back the bedclothes and put on a robe. One candle still burned, and she took it in a steady hand as she made her way from her room, down the stairs, and into Charles's sanctum.

She could feel him all about her. Every print, painting, book and ornament reminded her of him. They were the things he had chosen, and cared about; they were a part of him. When the light began to splutter she knew that she had no more time, and slowly she moved to the mahogany writing-desk under the window and opened the drawer.

* * *

The next day Bess went visiting in Highgate, not returning to town until nine o'clock. When she got back she found a note from Charles demanding she meet him that night in Covent Garden.

When she had woken that morning she had had a severe headache, but no recollection of what had happened the night before. She couldn't even recall getting undressed, or getting into bed. As she had drunk her coffee, she had thought about Adelaide and her condition, and had shrugged. What a fool she had been to be envious of the Austrian Romany. What if she were Charles's wife, and with child? He didn't love her.

She smiled, feeling very happy and alive. Charles couldn't wait until tomorrow, when they should have met; he needed her that very night.

She even laughed to herself at the terseness of his note. Passionate he may have been in bed, but a writer of love-letters he was not.

She put on a new dress, very fussy as she chose the right jewels to wear with it, and a perfume to intoxicate

Barron, making an excuse that Lady Jersey wanted to see her, so that Christine and Charmaine wouldn't be suspicious.

When she arrived at Covent Garden, Charles was not there, but she was quite content to sit and wait for him, thinking of what it would be like when he closed the door behind him and they were alone in their own private world.

He kept her waiting for thirty minutes, and when he strode into the dingy room Bess didn't see the icy rage in him at first.

"Dearest, so late. I thought perhaps you had forgotten you had sent for me. You can be so absent-minded."

He didn't speak, and then she noticed the riding-crop in his hand, and the hard, dreadful line of his mouth; the whiteness of his face.

A strange fear began to creep up from her silken slippers, making her knees weak. Whether it was the fact that it was night, or that Charles had such a terrifying look in his eyes, she didn't know, but suddenly she began to have flashes darting through her mind of what had taken place twelve hours before.

It was like the turning of pages in her memory: the rapid flutter of leaves, almost too quick to catch. She had been drunk; she knew that. But what else had she done? Why did she think all at once of paper and a quill? Had she written a letter: if so, to whom? Hadn't one of her servants, a boy, come into her room the night before, and hadn't she given him something?

She saw the piece of paper in Charles's hand, her heart sinking as he thrust it under her nose. She had been right: there had been a note.

"You wrote this." His voice was so soft, yet the venom in it seemed to fill the room. "You penned this, you bloody harpy. You let my wife know of our *affaire*, and in words which the basest foot-pad would hesitate to use."

"I can't remember!" She was panic-stricken by what she saw in him. "Charles, I truly can't. I wasn't myself. When you told me of the child I was so furious that I drank myself insensible."

"Not so insensible that you couldn't hold a pen."

"No, perhaps not." The dread in her

was increasing as the events of the previous night grew ominously clearer. "Perhaps I did write to Adelaide, but what I said I have no idea."

"Then I will read the letter to you, madam, and you will listen well." Still the whisper; still the dreadful, muted rage. "If, in truth, you have forgotten, I will remind you."

She tried to cover her ears when he was half-way through, sick shame flooding through her, but he wouldn't spare her a single syllable. Roughly, he jerked her arms down, forcing her to hear to the end.

"You bitch!" He flung the note away, his hand tightening on the whip. "You heartless, evil, scheming harlot."

"Charles, wait! I didn't know what I was doing. I told you: I had drunk too much. You have to believe me! I don't remember saying those things, truly."

"Don't make matters worse by lying."

"I'm not, I'm not! Charles, please! I wouldn't have done such a thing if I'd been sober, you know that. But I'll tell Adelaide it was a lie. I'll say anything you like, but don't look at me like that.

What did she say?"

"She didn't say anything." The heat had gone out of him and he was ice-cold once more. "Not a thing."

"You mean that . . . that she just shewed you the note, and said nothing?"

"No, she didn't shew it to me. I found it in her hand, and she was not able to say anything, because she had taken my pistol and shot herself through the heart."

"Oh my God!"

Bess almost fainted, holding on to the chair to steady herself. It had never occurred to her that Adelaide really cared for Charles: it had been a marriage of convenience, or so Bess had thought. What must the girl have made of that letter, with its crude obscenities which Barron had mouthed, as if the words were burning his tongue.

"She's . . . dead?"

"Yes, people do die with a bullet in their heart, and you killed her as surely as if you had fired the gun yourself."

"But . . . I had no idea . . . oh, believe me . . . I hadn't any idea! I've told you I have no recollection of what I wrote last night, nor did I think Adelaide cared a fig for you. If I'd been sober . . ." She paused, her eyes dilating. "Charles! You didn't care for her, did you? You didn't love her?"

"No, but she was my wife, and you are responsible for her death and that of my child, and you will live to regret it."

She saw his right hand move, but wasn't quick enough to get out of the way. The crop bit into her, and she gasped, stumbling away from the chair in an effort to avoid the next blow, but it was useless. Barron tore the cloak from her shoulders and threw her over the bed.

"Well, madam," he said in the same ghastly whisper. "You've had your fun. Now you will pay for it."

She didn't scream or cry out once. She bit the pillow hard, taking the punishment without a sound. Even when he had slammed out of the room, and she was left holding her sore and aching body, she didn't blame Charles.

Whether she remembered it or not, she had done a dreadful thing, and she had deserved what she got. It was the kind of justice which she had learned in the slums, and had never forgotten. The slightest wrong-doing had brought an instant flogging from her father in its wake; it was no different now. A sin meant painful retribution.

No different from the old days, except that now Charles would never speak to her again. Whatever sort of feeling he had had for her would now be dead; as dead as Adelaide.

She managed to get to her feet, picking the cloak up and wrapping it tightly round her, so that the coachman would not see the torn and stained gown, trying to tidy her ruffled hair with fingers which wouldn't stop shaking. It would be hard to conceal what had happened from Christine and Charmaine, but somehow she would have to do it.

What had taken place was between herself and Charles. It was as much their secret as the sexual fulfilment they had shared before.

As she reached the door, Bess paused, looking back to the room which she would never see again.

"I'm sorry, Charles," she whispered.

"Truly sorry. Dear God, I wish you believed me."

* * *

With Adelaide buried, and the scandal hushed up, Charles Barron became more dissolute than ever. Tales were told of his suicidal rides between London and Brighton. He drank too much; he gambled so carelessly that Brummell, and even the prince, remonstrated with him.

"There won't be a penny of Adelaide's money left if you go on like this." Brummell was sauntering towards White's, blandly ignoring the fawning smiles of those passing by. "No one likes a game of chance more than I, but what you are doing is pure madness. What are you trying to do? Kill yourself?"

"Why not?" Charles was like granite; no one could reach him. "A short life and a gay one, eh?"

"Very short, at the rate you are going." Brummell hesitated, knowing how sore the wound was. "Not my business, of course, but she wouldn't have wanted this."

"Adelaide?"

"Yes. She was very fond of you. She would be deeply grieved by what you are doing."

"Fond of me!" Charles gave a short laugh. "Yes, I suppose she was."

"One day, perhaps, you'll be able to talk about it." The Beau paused outside White's. "More to it than people were told, I know that. I won't pry, but when you need someone . . . "

Barron nodded.

"Good of you, George, but there's nothing to talk about. It's over."

The Beau sighed.

"As you will. Shall we go in, and in the name of heaven don't go above ten thousand."

But Barron did, and lost, and lost again finding himself back with 'Jew' King the next morning.

"Twenty thousand, sir?" The money-lender's shrewd eyes moved over Barron's haggard face and thin, straight lips. "Can't do more than that."

The whole of society knew that Barron was riding roughshod along the road to hell and were enjoying the spectacle.

Bess listened to the tales of his nights spent with Cyprians, his obsession with the cards, the dangerous racing at breakneck speed, and the brandy which would be the end of him, so everyone said, were he not to stop.

She felt numb inside, as if she had stopped living, but there was nothing she could do. Charles wouldn't have consented to see her, even if she could have found the courage to face him.

Since everyone believed that she and Charles disliked each other, she could only feign an outward satisfaction that he was hurtling along the road to disaster, but Christine and Charmaine shook their heads at each other when they heard Bess's heartbroken sobs through her locked door.

It was then that she found that she too was with child, and the world seemed to crash about her ears. She couldn't tell Charles, for he had rebuffed her on the previous occasion, and now, despising her as he did, there was no hope at all that he would help.

She made a full confession to Christine and Charmaine, since it was impossible to conceal the truth from them, and she knew that her secret was safe with them.

"We shall have to leave London," she said, dry-eyed and in full possession again. "I have purchased a house in Surrey, and we shall move next week."

"But the baby?" Christine couldn't bear the unhappiness she saw in Bess. "What will happen when it is born?"

"No one will know, for the house is in a secluded part. Later, we shall say that it is my cousin's, who died at its birth, and that I have undertaken to raise it as my own. Never speak of this to anyone, or let a soul know where we are going."

They murmured instant agreement, but when they had gone Bess's hands were clenched together in torment. Away from London and Charles. Even though she hadn't seen him since that awful night, she had the sense of him being near, but once away from the capital even that consolation would be lost.

Suddenly she sat up straight, colour draining from her face as another thought struck her. What if Charles in a drunken state were to let slip some hint of the origins of the Countess of Crayford? Her departure from London would cause comment enough: if anyone were to ask Charles for his opinion as to why she had gone, and, if he were intoxicated, he might tell his eager audience about Bess from the slums. Certainly, drunk or sober, he hated her enough now to ruin her.

The thought kept her awake at nights, but finally she forced herself to stop worrying. This was no time to be frightened, not with the child on its way. Besides, Bess Hathaway was made of sterner stuff; not a weakling like Adelaide Barron who hadn't been able to stand the truth.

In her position Bess would have fought back and given her husband a right rousting, tearing the eyes out of her rival's head into the bargain.

Bess closed her lids, the familiar ache returning once more. If only she hadn't been so angry that night, so that she had sought forgetfulness in a bottle. But for that, the letter wouldn't have been written, and Adelaide would still be alive. Then, she, Bess, and Charles would still have those few precious hours together each week. True, she would have had to accept that another woman would bear Charles's heir, but one could grow used to anything in time, that is, if one's heart were not breaking.

When everything was packed, and the house ready to be closed, Bess took herself off to Clarges Street. 'Jew' King was astonished to see the slim woman, dressed in black, for normally it was the young bucks with no sense in their heads who came seeking his help. He ushered the woman to a chair, trying to see her face, but it was too heavily veiled. He took his seat behind the desk and waited.

When she spoke, it was in a very low voice, as if she didn't want him to know who she was, and, indeed, she made it clear at once that the matter was of great secrecy.

"Of course, madam, of course. You can trust me, for I am the recipient of many confidences. Too much faro, was it?"

"Faro?"

"Why yes, Lost at the tables, did you?"

"No."

'Jew' King leaned back and considered his unusual visitor. Although he could see nothing of her, for even her hands were gloved, he knew instinctively that she was beautiful. It was inherent in her carriage, and in the graceful way in which she had sat down.

"Then . . . ?"

"It is difficult to explain." The words were lower than ever. "I beg you not to ask questions but to do what I ask. I will pay generously for your services, of course."

That was encouraging, and he nodded.

"It will be my pleasure. What service can I be to you?"

She didn't answer at once, opening a large reticule and laying out a handful of necklaces, brooches, ear-rings, bracelets and hair ornaments which dazzled him. He didn't need to examine them closely to realise their value: there was a fortune in front of him, and he pulled his lower lip in perturbation.

"What is it I am to do, madam?"

"Sell them. They are worth a lot, aren't they?"

"Indeed they are, but I'm not the man to come to for such a service. I'm a money-lender."

"I know, and that is what I want you to do: lend money."

He frowned, hitching his chair closer.

"My wits must be deserting me today, for if these are yours, as I assume they are, why do you need to borrow money?"

She hesitated, and he said softly:

"Like a priest, I am. Any secret is safe with me. If it weren't so, I wouldn't have a customer in London."

"No, I suppose not, and I have to trust you." The woman touched the emerald necklace nearest to her. "Sell these for as much as you can get, and take your fee. The rest you are to lend to Charles Barron when he comes to you for help."

King cleared his throat.

"Sir Charles, eh? You know him then?"

"Yes."

"A friend in need."

"He does not think of me as a friend, but that is not important. Will you do this for me?"

"Yes, but at the rate Sir Charles is going these days even this lot won't last for long. Some say he is losing his mind."

"Perhaps he has reason." The head bowed, and the fingers were tight on the black silk cloak. "And that is another confidence I must put in your hands, Mr King. I am leaving London to-day, but no one knows where I am going, and no one must, except you."

"Yes?"

"When the money has gone, let me know. I will arrange for you to have more."

"Sir Charles is a lucky man."

He thought the woman might be crying, but he wasn't sure.

"No, he is the most unfortunate creature alive."

He pressed no more, accepting her address and bowing her out. Then he went back to the desk and examined the pile of gems. Suddenly he frowned. One brooch, of unusual design, caught his attention, and he stared at it for a long while. The Crayford diamonds were famous, and this was one of the best pieces in the collection.

He was uneasy for a second or two, wondering if his unknown visitor had come by the jewellery honestly.

He did nothing that day, but on the following afternoon he made a few discreet enquiries. His informant was quite adamant when 'Jew' King expressed disbelief.

"S'right, Mr King, the countess as gorn. Off yesterday, without a word to no one.'Ouse all locked up; no servants left neither."

King hummed to himself for a moment, then dismissed the man. The Countess of Crayford who, or so he had learned, had no time for Charles Barron had provided enough to keep that gentleman in reasonable solvency for at least six months, provided he didn't bet it all against the turn of a card. And when that money was gone, more would be available.

It was a tantalising puzzle, but King was not in the business of solving riddles. Whatever reasons, it was her own affair, and as long as she paid his fees it was nothing to him. He brushed the matter aside and got on with his work.

* * *

A few months in seclusion made a world of difference to Bess. She slept and ate, and walked in the gardens of Risborough Lodge, a small Elizabethan manor, several miles from its nearest neighbour.

Gradually her guilt and misery melted away. She had done a bad thing, but she hadn't been responsible for her actions at the time, and had had no idea that Adelaide loved Charles. She even managed to convince herself that it was mostly Charles's fault. He should have made excuses not to go to his wife's bed. He shouldn't have given her, Bess, a reason to drown such rage and pain.

Nevertheless, Risborough Lodge soon felt like a prison, and Bess decided to move, this time to Kent, where she had neighbours. They were well-to-do, but had never moved amongst the élite of London, and she was able to call herself Mrs Charles, a recent widow, and not be suspected. She told no one of her departure, quite forgetting 'Jew'

King, settling down to await the birth of the baby.

The worry that Charles might expose her had quite gone. He hadn't done so so far, and there was no reason to think he would do so in the future. Whatever else, he was a man of honour. She had paid the price for his silence once, and she doubted that he would break his word now. He would have money to gamble with, and buy fine clothes. "And pay a few strumpets to warm his bed," said Bess sourly to herself.

But even that thought faded when her son was born. She stared in wonderment at the tiny thing in her arms. He was so like Charles that it made her catch her breath. She told herself it was because she wanted the boy to look like his father that she believed it so, but when Christine Cotter peeped at the mite, she cried aloud.

"Oh, what a pet, and how like Sir Charles. No one could mistake it, even though he is but a few hours old. What name shall we have?"

"Charles, like his father." Her joy faded as she looked up at Christine.

"Like the father who won't give him a name."

"But Sir Charles doesn't know about him."

"Do you suppose it would make any difference if he did?" Bess was caustic. "I know him better than you."

"But he might be willing to marry you, now that he is . . . well . . . free."

"I doubt if he will ever marry again, but I tell you this." Bess's mouth was like a vice. "If he should ever try to wed another, with my son unacknowledged, I'll stop the marriage, no matter what price has to be paid. If Sir Charles wants to take a wife again it'll be me, and no one else."

"But . . . " Christine shuddered. There was something almost abnormal in her friend's eyes. "As I say, he doesn't know about the boy."

"And that's how it'll stay, unless I hear of him talking of nuptials again. Christine, we need someone to keep us informed of what is going on in London. I was sorry when Mr Burnham wouldn't come with us, but now I see it was for the best. He can be our ears and eyes, for he dearly likes to listen to gossip. Write to him and tell him I want a weekly letter sent by a fast chaise. Everything that's going on I need to know about, especially if it concerns Sir Charles Barron. I've paid my debt to him in more ways than you know, Christine. The sheet's wiped clean now, and we're even. Let him try to cheat me again, and I'll make him sorry he was ever born."

The worried Christine tiptoed out, and Bess looked back at her infant.

"I've got to hate him, precious, don't you see? If I can't do that, he'll break me, for I love him so. Oh, Charlie, Charlie, I do love him so."

7

TEN months after Bess had left London, Charles Barron presented himself at the home of Augusta FitzCromer, Duchess of Merton.

The money which Bess had left with 'Jew' King had soon gone, and since that worthy gentleman had failed to receive a response from Bess at the address she had given him, he had shrugged, and consigned Barron to his just fate.

King knew that the beautiful Countess of Crayford had vanished as mysteriously as she had arrived on the social scene, but he wasn't concerned. He only cared about her money, and since that was no longer available, he dismissed her from his mind.

Not so Beau Barron. Pursuing an almost lunatic path of self-destruction, Charles couldn't get her out of his thoughts. She haunted him by day, and he dreamt about her by night. He cursed her for what she was doing to him, for he had never before allowed any woman to become of real consequence to him.

He drank more heavily, gambled more madly, drove his carriages faster, and, as if to punish himself for Adelaide's death, slept only with the lowest of common prostitutes.

His friends remonstrated with him, even the prince, now Regent, shaking his head.

"Want to take care, Charles. Like a bit of a gamble myself, and nothin' wrong with havin' a woman or two, but . . . "

Brummell was blunter still.

"You look appalling," he told Charles as they dined at White's with Alvanley, Lord Worcester and 'Poodle' Byng. "I swear that coat positively hangs on you like a sack. Why don't you eat properly?"

Barron glanced down at his untouched plate.

"Waste of time."

"You don't regard drinking as a waste of time."

"That's different." A touch of Charles's old humour crept out. "Are you trying to mother me?"

"God forbid!" Brummell sipped his

wine with reflective pleasure. "Leave that to Augusta."

The smile was gone from Barron's face.

"Augusta. Yes."

"Goin' to accept her offer?"

"I'm not sure. Only in the last resort, for I can't stand the woman."

But the last resort came, and when Barron was faced with an overwhelming gambling debt which had to be paid without delay, there was nothing for it but a visit to the large house in one of London's most fashionable squares.

On his way there, he thought about Adelaide, and then about Bess. He felt as empty as a gourd, as if life had already left him, and he was dragging another man's body around. Brummell had been right. He had lost weight. The cheeks were sharper, the hollows beneath them deeper. There were new lines etched round his mouth, and his eyes were like those of a corpse.

He had stopped blaming Bess for Adelaide's suicide. Bess had said she hadn't been sober when she wrote the note he had found, and he believed her when cooler counsels prevailed. Whatever else Bess was, she wasn't spiteful in that way. She would never have inflicted such an injury had she been herself. In any event, it was his fault far more than hers. If he and Bess hadn't been lovers, Bess couldn't have written the letter at all.

He wondered where she was; the slender, lovely woman with jewel eyes, who could twist his soul, and make his heart ache. No one knew: there wasn't the faintest whisper of where she had gone, although he had made discreet enquiries many times.

He was shewn into the duchess's drawing-room, a place as formidable as its owner. If he married Augusta, and there seemed no other way out of his present predicament, he would be master of the palatial house, including the priceless paintings, the gold and silver ornaments, the crystal, and the well-tended furniture. His mouth turned down at the corners. Of course he wouldn't be master, at least, only in name. The duchess would control her possessions, just as she did now, only in future she would have him under her thumb too, dictating her will to him as if he were one of her flunkeys. He had no illusions about Augusta.

She swept into the room looking far more regal than any royalty, wearing a white muslin gown with a train, and a diamond tiara which could have settled all Barron's debts with ease.

"My dear Charles, how very nice to see you. You are ten minutes late, but we will say no more of that now. Just remember in future that I do not like to be kept waiting. If I say ten o'clock, that is just what I mean."

Barron took a deep breath.

Augusta was fifty if she were a day, her skin beginning to wrinkle, her black eyes not made more attractive by the heavy bags formed beneath them. Her mouth was small and pinched, her nose a trifle too dominant. For a second Charles had a sudden vision of Bess, and almost turned and made for the door, but it was no good. Bess and he could only hurt each other. Augusta couldn't hurt him, because she couldn't reach him. Also, she was excessively rich.

The duchess had seated herself by the fireplace, a hand heavy with rings directing Charles to take a place opposite her.

"Now, there are certain things to settle between us before we decide the date of the wedding." She was brisk and business-like. "You will understand, I am sure, that your present mode of life will have to stop at once. You have become the most notorious rake in London."

He gazed at her bleakly. She really was the most hideous of women, and the line of her lips boded no good for him.

"Your gambling must cease. I do not mind you playing a game of faro now and then, but only when I am with you, to ensure that you do not lose your head. As for your drinking, that too must be checked, for you are killing yourself, I do declare, with so much brandy and wine. I will judge how much you may have each day, and not a drop more will you get. And as to women . . . "

Charles was hardly listening to Augusta's terms. He had known in advance the kind of price she would exact for marriage, and his rescue from bankruptcy and dishonour. She had no feelings for him: she merely wanted a tame lap-dog to follow her about and pick up a dropped fan or lace kerchief.

But in that Barron was entirely wrong. As Augusta laid out her terms with crisp clarity, no one, and certainly not Charles, could have guessed what was surging beneath her flat bosom.

She had fallen in love with Charles the first time she had seen him, loathing the timid Austrian wench who had secured the place in Barron's bed which she, Augusta, so longed to fill. Even now, ill and pale, he was so handsome that she almost rose to clasp him to her, and tell him how much she cared for him, but that, of course, would never do. If he should once guess her devotion, which, she admitted herself, was as silly as a sixteen-year-old's, he would have the upper hand, and she had no intention of allowing that to happen. But . . . oh . . . his eyes made her almost dizzy, and the pain round his mouth made her want to comfort him like a child.

She pulled herself together. She was getting quite maudlin and absurd. If she wasn't careful Charles would begin to suspect. Her determination to conceal her true feelings made her tarter than ever.

"There will be no other women. It may be *de rigueur* amongst your friends to take a mistress or two, but once you are my husband you can put aside such thoughts, for I will not tolerate adultery in you, either with your own kind or with these wretched street girls you seem to favour. Do you understand me? Charles! Are you listening?"

"Yes, yes, I'm listening."

And he was now, heart sinking as the shrill voice rose another note or two. How was he going to bear this woman, scrawny and old and strident, the sap in her veins dried up, her mind as rigid as a bar of iron?

"I hope you are, for I'll have no nonsense from you, Charles Barron. I'll settle your debts, however high they are, and make you an allowance which I consider should be sufficient for your needs. For your part, you will eschew your wild life, and settle down to your duties as my spouse."

Their eyes met across the room. Augusta was hot with excitement inside at the thought of their wedding-night.

Her frigid exterior was no guide to the urgent sexual needs which had killed off two previous husbands and left her wholly unsatisfied. Charles was picturing that night too, but he was filled with dread. Augusta, as a wife; a nagging, demanding harridan, who held the purse-strings. He began to wonder whether death were not preferable to a life-long sentence with the duchess.

"Well, that is agreed. Now you may kiss me, and then I shall make the necessary arrangements."

"For the wedding?"

"Of course." Her eyes snapped angrily. "What do you think we have been talking about?"

"The wedding." He bit his lip, wishing with all his heart that he didn't have to ask the next question. "And my debts? Can they be met soon?"

Her mouth moved in a satisfied smile.

"Of course." Yes, she really had got him where she wanted him, and his tone had been almost humble. For a second she frowned. She hoped that he wouldn't be humble in bed. She had had two such milksops to contend with already. During the day she wanted to give the orders; at night she wanted a man who could master her. "Yes, my dear, they'll be attended to. Now, a kiss to seal the bargain."

He rose, intending to touch her cheek lightly, but she turned her head unexpectedly, and her kiss against his mouth was firm and demanding. He felt her tongue force itself between his lips and was shocked. He hadn't expected this. Like everyone else, he had believed Augusta to be a prude, but she wasn't. He was far too experienced in dealing with women to misunderstand her salutation, and it sickened him. To live with her would be bad enough; to have to make that kind of love to her would be almost intolerable.

He didn't mention the last incident to his friends when they met together on the following evening, confining himself to a recital of Augusta's other requirements.

"No drink, no gambling, no women."

Alvanley gave a grunt.

"She's a hard woman, it's true, but . . . "

" . . . devilishly rich," finished Worcester

gloomily. “Terrible choice to have to make, Charles, but at least she’ll pay your debts.”

“And take more than a pound of flesh in return.” Barron was filled with despondency. He had had time to consider what life with Augusta was really going to be like, and he almost shuddered. “It will be like a prison.”

“A silken one though.” Brummell took a pinch of snuff from a cloisonné box, using one hand only, with a grace peculiar to himself. “Nothing is free in this life, m’dear. Face it, what choice have you got?”

“None.” Barron shrugged. “It’s Augusta, or dishonour.”

The others murmured in sympathy. It was a wretched decision to have to make.

“At least she won’t wear you out like the last two husbands she had. Got far too old for that sort of thing, if you know what I mean.”

Charles glanced at ‘Poodle’ Byng, keeping his face blank.

“Quite,” he said, after a pause. “That is at least one consolation. Now, let’s forget Augusta for to-night. Since she has not yet settled my dues, I shall gamble for the highest stakes I can, and she can pay for that too, if I lose."

They rose, making for the tables. As he sat down, ready to play, Charles gave one last sight.

What would Bess think of him if she knew what he was about to do? Her scorn would be no greater than his own self-disgust, but thank God Bess didn't know yet. And when she did find out, it would be too late. He would be Augusta FitzCromer's husband.

* * *

"Do you hear what I'm saying, Christine?" Bess was ablaze with temper, cheeks pink, eyes like daggers. "Roger says in this letter that Charles is to marry the Duchess of Merton. That dried-up old crone! Everyone thinks she's so prim and proper, but I know better. It takes a woman, and one like me, to know the truth. She's hot for him, the loathsome bag! She wants him in her bed, and she's prepared to pay for it."

"It may not be true." Miss Cotter saw the misery behind the tirade. "It could be just a rumour."

"No, it's real enough. Too much detail in Roger's note for that. The date's fixed too, and Charles's gambling debts are to be taken care of. Oh, how could he! How could he!"

"Perhaps he hadn't anywhere else to turn." Christine tried to defend Charles as best she could. "Remember Mr Burnham's last two letters have told of the losses he has sustained."

"Yes, but he had money . . . "

Bess broke off, one hand pressed against her lips in consternation. She had quite forgotten to tell 'Jew' King when she had moved to Kent. Charles would have soon borrowed the proceeds of the jewels she had left, and King wouldn't have been able to reach her to tell her that more money was needed.

"Yes?" Christine was looking at her enquiringly. "You were saying?"

"Nothing." Bess dismissed the matter with a shake of the head. Even if Barron had been in dire straits, marriage with Augusta FitzCromer was really too outrageous. "It's nothing, but I'll stop Charles's tricks. I'll make sure he doesn't get to the altar with that old . . . "

She was as good as her word, and Augusta, some few days later, read the missive in her hand, staring now and then at the baby which the nervous nursemaid held in her arms. There was no doubt that what the letter said was true. It was Charles's son, right enough. Even though the infant was so young, there was no mistaking the likeness.

Her lips clamped together as she screwed the note up and flung it away.

"Get that bastard out of my house," she screeched. "Do you hear me? Take it back to its mother, whoever she is, and tell her not to let it soil my doorstep again. Get out! Get out!"

The maid, terrified by the maniacal fury of the noblewoman, was only too glad to obey. She rushed out of the house, clutching her precious bundle, running helter-skelter round the corner to where Bess's carriage waited.

"For Gawd's sake, let's get 'ome," she said to the coachman, and sank back on the seat with relief. "Thought the old tartar were goin' to kill me, and the bairn too. Never seen nothin' like it, and that's a fact. Wonder what made 'er so fierce. Wonder, too, why missus told me to bring Master Charlie 'ere in the first place."

"None of yer business, me girl," replied the coachman, and picked up the reins. "Not yours to be pryin' into what yer betters do, so jest shut yer bone-box and let's git 'ome."

The interview between Augusta and Charles was stormy. At first he had no idea what she was talking about, but the duchess had retrieved Bess's letter and thrust it into his hand.

"Read that!" shouted Augusta, red with frustrated wrath. Charles wasn't going to get off lightly for this. "Do you deny the child's yours? No, don't bother to do so, for I saw the wretched brat with my own eyes. It's yours right enough. Damn you! How dare you let your whore send her spawn here to my house?"

Charles said nothing. His ire was as great as Augusta's, but it was under better control. Bess had done this. He had had no idea that she was with child, and she hadn't thought fit to tell him. Not only that, she was vindictive enough to stop his one chance of solvency. His earlier judgment of her character had been wrong. She was spiteful enough for anything.

"I will deal with it," he said abruptly. "Augusta, I would ask your forgiveness, but I knew nothing about this."

"I can believe it," she spat back. "The manner of your life is such that you have doubtless been responsible for a dozen or so bastards. If we marry, there'll be no more of that."

"If?" He looked up quickly. There was, it seemed, still a chance for him, but he would have to be very wary. "You mean to end our betrothal because of this?"

"And why not, pray?" She twitched her skirts away from him, as if he were unclean. "Do you imagine I enjoyed receiving a letter like that?"

"No, of course not." He moved cautiously, his blind anger checked temporarily as he took steps to placate the enraged duchess. He could deal with

Bess later; now he had to coax this termagent into forgiveness. It wouldn't be easy, but he needed her money, and pride and repugnance would have to be put aside.

"But you knew what I was like." He forced his voice to be penitent. "Yes, I have lived a loose and immoral life, but all that would have changed with you, my dear, you know that."

"Do I indeed?"

She had not relented an inch.

"Yes, you do. You set the terms, and I agreed."

"Just to get your bills paid, sir. Once that was done no doubt you'd go rolling in the stews again with never a thought for me."

Barron gritted his teeth. It had to be done, however nauseating it would be. Words were not going to win this battle for him, and a victory he had to have, and by now he knew the measure of Augusta.

He took three steps across the room, and, ignoring her shriek of protest, caught her in his arms and kissed her hard on the lips.

"Enough!" He was sharp, his fingers bruising her wrist. "Be quiet, Augusta. You've said enough."

She paused, eyes almost closed. Oh yes, Charles was going to be a most satisfactory lover, and, after all, what did one more bastard in the world matter. Even the graphic description of Charles's capabilities in bed, penned by an unknown harlot, was forgotten.

"Very well," she murmured, almost meekly. "Kiss me again, my love, and we'll say no more about it."

"That's better." Barron had to steel himself to touch her a second time. "As you say, we'll talk no more about it."

His hand wandered down her arm, making her shiver with delight, and his lip curled unseen. Good enough: and after this Augusta could loosen her purse-strings, for, in the name of the Virgin, he'd earned every penny she was going to pay.

* * *

It took Barron a week to find Roger Burnham, and less than three minutes to force the truth of Bess's whereabouts out of him.

"She was so good to me," wept the shattered Burnham, "and I've betrayed her because I was afraid of being hurt."

"Don't whine." Barron was scathing. "If you'd cared that much about her you wouldn't have worried about a broken arm or jaw."

"I'm old."

"You're a coward. Don't lie to yourself, or to me either. Besides, she's not worth it."

Bess was in the garden when Barron arrived at the mellow old farmhouse set against a small copse, with a stream running along one side. It was very peaceful, and he could smell damp grass and burning wood, checking his horses and bringing them to a standstill.

He leapt from his seat, striding along the narrow path, pausing at the heavy wooden door. Then he heard Bess singing, and turned on his heel, making for the rose-bushes from whence the sound came.

She didn't realise he was there until he was almost on top of her, and before she could compose herself his scalding fury was pouring all over her like molten lead.

"You bloody bitch!" His hand was like steel on her arm. "I ought to cut your damned throat, but why should I pay the consequences of that? You're not worth it, as I told your spy, Burnham."

Bess was pale, but after the first fearful moment she had herself in hand. She was shocked, not by his anger, which she had expected to descend upon her eventually, but by his appearance. He looked so thin; almost ill.

For his part, Barron's bad temper was heightened by the very sight of Bess. The low-cut dress allowed ample scope for a study of her gently swelling breasts and long slender neck. The sun had hardly touched the wonderful skin, and her mouth was more tempting than even he had remembered it.

"You bawd! You unspeakable, filthy strumpet! How dare you interfere with my life in this way?"

Bess was entirely herself now, not even wincing at the increasing pressure of her arm.

"But why not, sir? You interfered with mine. Our son is ample proof of that."

"Why didn't you tell me you were with child?"

She mocked.

"And have you say what you said before? 'Take this money until you can go whoring again.' Oh no, my dear, I wasn't going to give you that satisfaction twice."

He was side-tracked.

"I wouldn't have said that."

"Yes you would, or something equally wounding."

"You can't be sure."

"No, not now, but it doesn't matter, does it?" Her smile grew sweeter and more devastating. "What did dear Augusta make of my Charlie? I hope she loved him as much as I do. Indeed, why shouldn't she, seeing he favours you so much?"

When he struck her across the face she didn't flicker so much as an eye-lash.

"Your answer to everything, isn't it?"

He heard the edge under her low tone, but ignored it.

"A beating for an impudent doxy?

Yes, I suppose it is. It hasn't failed before."

"But it will fail now, Charles Barron; make no mistake about that." Bess's smile was gone. "You've abused me for the very last time."

"You think so?" His sneer was as cutting as his tongue. "You could be wrong. And you've something to answer for. I may not soil my hands on you again, but I'll make you rue what you've done. By to-morrow night all London will know you for what you are. I shall tell them."

She smoothed her sleeve, his hold on her gone.

"I don't think you will."

She was picking up her straw basket, half-filled with flowers which made him think of his childhood. Summers spent in Shropshire, with ice and snow in winter, and hot, hot sun and blooms to scent the air in spring and summer.

"Oh, why not?"

"Has the duchess paid your bills yet?"

"None of your business."

"It is, as you will see. Has she, Charles?"

He hesitated, wondering what she was up to.

"Not yet, but she will."

"Not if I write to her again, or even go and see her. I could tell her other things about our nights together which would make that hateful old biddy sick to her stomach. I'll tell her that you love me."

"She wouldn't believe you, and it's not true anyway."

Her smile was back; very feline.

"I could convince her it is so, never doubt it."

"You are a wicked, heartless cow." He bit the words off like wire threads. "You said that you wrote to Adelaide when you were drunk and didn't know what you were doing. Now, I doubt that. I think you set out to kill her."

Bess stiffened. She had often lain awake at nights and thought about Adelaide. Poor, helpless Adelaide, ground between the millstones of the destructive love of two other people.

"That is not true. I was intoxicated. You know full well that I would never have . . . "

"Shut up!" He slashed his riding-boot

with his crop. "I don't want to listen to any more lies, and lies they are, for have you not just threatened my future again?"

"In a way, I suppose, but my mind is not yet made up."

"Then you have had a change of heart?" His brows met. "You will not write to Augusta, or try to see her?"

"Certainly I will, if you expose me."

They were moving further away from the house, Bess turning to him, her expression bringing him up short. She was up to something new; he could tell, because he knew her so well.

"Yes? What now?"

She laughed softly.

"We are well matched, aren't we? So alike, my dear, and that is what I want to talk to you about. A bargain between us."

"What kind of bargain?" He was more doubtful than ever, wondering what she would say if he took her in his arms and kissed her, as he longed to do. Even when she infuriated him to the point of madness, he still wanted her with every fibre of his being. "What sort of offer can you make?"

The emerald eyes were like the stones they resembled: cold and brilliant.

"Marry me, and give our son a name. I'll pay your debts, and no strings. You can gamble, drink, kill yourself on the road to Brighton. I won't stop you."

"And go whoring at night?"

He saw her instinctive reaction, and drove the rapier in.

"No, you wouldn't like that, would you? You're just like Augusta. You want a tame pet, and you want revenge."

"If you read Augusta that way, you're not the man I took you for." She was ironic. "She lusts after you as much as any bitch on heat."

"Be quiet!" He was violent again. "I'm going to marry Augusta."

"I've told you; she won't have you, when I've done talking." One hand rested on his for a brief second. "We could manage, you and I. I need a husband, you need money. What do you say?"

"I say go to perdition, and take your ill-gotten money with you."

Charles left her standing there, the basket spilling its contents on to the grass, leaping into his curricle as Bess turned sadly back to the house. She had made her play, and it hadn't worked. Now he hated her more than ever: hated her enough to marry the FitzCromer woman, just to spite her.

"Damn him," she said to her wide-eyed, uncomprehending infant. "Oh, Charlie, damn him, damn him!"

* * *

A week later Barron returned to Kent. Bess received him without surprise, begging him to be seated, and offering him refreshment.

"Thank you, no."

He was short, brushing her offer aside. The last few days had been a disaster. Knowing Bess meant every word of what she had said, there was no escape from his problems by marriage with Augusta.

That left two other possible routes of escape. A turning of his luck at the tables, or an acceptance of Bess's offer.

But luck wasn't with him, and to his already crippling debts he had managed to add another five thousand in one night, and a further seven thousand the next.

That left Bess's offer. He didn't know why the thought of it made him sick at heart. She was young, beautiful, enormously rich, and the mother of his son, but she was buying him, as she would buy a necklace or a stallion. It was utterly degrading, and every second of their interview was like a wound being probed.

"I'm glad you've seen reason," she said smoothly, concealing the relief which made her want to reach out and touch him. "We shall deal famously together, you'll see."

"No doubt, madam." He was stony, and quickly built a barrier between them which he intended should not be pulled down. The very sight of her was a taunt. Her body which he craved, her face which was imprinted indelibly on his mind. The woman he knew he would always need, no matter how much they tried to injure each other: the woman who had just paid good cash for him. "I am sure we shall manage to live a civilised existence together."

She nodded, chilled by his response.

He didn't want her for herself; he never had. He was only accepting her offer now because there was no other way open to him. She had just closed the last one, and removed the Duchess of Merton from his life. It wasn't going to be easy.

"Do you want to see the boy?"

"Not particularly." The lids were half-closed, so that she couldn't see what was in his eyes. "Another time, perhaps. After all, there will be plenty of opportunities, won't there?"

Another blow, more painful than any his whip could inflict, but she inclined her head, totally poised.

"As you wish. Will you make the arrangements for the wedding, or shall I?"

"Oh, you, madam, for it seems to me that you have a positive genius for arranging things, and mostly to my disadvantage. Yes, by all means, you forge the links of my fetters, and let me know when the end of my freedom is to take place."

She swallowed hard, but she wouldn't let him see what he was doing to her.

"Very well. Please leave a note of what

accommodation you need. I will see to that too."

"I'm sure you will." He got up, looking at her in contempt. "I hope you'll think I'm worth the sum you've got to pay for me."

"I have no doubt of it." Her chin was up, but she prayed he would go soon, for she knew that she was at breaking-point. "I've always had a good eye for a bargain."

"Good-day." His bow was perfunctory, almost insulting. "Until we meet in church." The line of his mouth was frightening. "And don't think you'll pay in gold alone, for I can assure you that you won't. I'll make you regret what you've done, you may rely on that."

It was at least fifteen minutes after he had gone before Bess began to cry. She had been too frozen by his obvious disgust for the blessed relief of tears to start. She had won, but at what a price?

She turned her head and looked out over the darkening fields.

"Oh, Charles," she whispered, as she reached for her handkerchief. "Oh, my love, my love, what have I done?"

8

THE ensuing four months were the longest in Bess's life, or so it seemed to her.

The whole of society had been agog when Augusta, Duchess of Merton, had packed her goods and chattels and left for Italy, saying that she would never again return to a land where so many barbarous people lived. The collective amazement grew when news filtered through to London that Beau Barron and the Countess of Crayford had been married in a tiny village church in Essex, with no one to witness this remarkable event save an elderly seamstress and a few bucolic passers-by who had strayed in out of curiosity. There was no talk of them returning to London, so the rumour had said: the Beau and his lady were going to settle down to a peaceful pastoral existence.

The peace, and the pastoral existence, lasted for a very short time, for Barron grew so bored that Bess could see the only solution was to go back to the capital. She dreaded the thought, not only because of wagging tongues, and the questions which she didn't want to answer, but because of the temptations open to Charles.

With her customary efficiency, she arranged the purchase of a house off Grosvenor Square, travelling to town to ensure that its furnishing and decoration were perfect, and that there was a first-class staff to run their new home.

She left her son with Christine Cotter and Charles, for the latter had announced firmly that he had no intention of becoming involved in the choice of curtain material, or the engagement of kitchen-maids.

Now and then Barron went into the light, airy room where his son lay, gurgling at the ceiling. He tried to choose occasions when Miss Cotter was not about, but wasn't always successful.

"Isn't he beautiful?" Christine beamed at her charge, as proud as Bess herself of the sturdy boy. "See, Sir Charles, how intelligent he looks, and he is the very mirror-image of you."

She bent and picked the baby up, and before he knew what was happening Barron was holding the warm bundle in his arms, looking down at the smooth pink cheeks and large knowing eyes. It was a sensation he had never felt before. His own son: his flesh and blood. Bess's flesh and blood.

"Take him," he said finally to Miss Cotter, "and don't tell your mistress about this."

"But, sir, she would be so pleased to know that . . . "

"You heard me." The hooded gaze was intimidating. "She is not to know."

"Very well, but . . . "

"Stop your clacking, woman, or I shall find out, and then you will be extremely sorry."

Once they had returned to London Barron picked up his old life as if he had never left it. Occasionally Bess would accompany him to a ball or soirée, and it was with mixed feelings that he watched men's heads turn as they gazed admiringly at her. Motherhood had enriched her, giving her a mantle of gentle serenity, and no one ever guessed the turmoil of her heart as she mouthed polite phrases, and made her curtsey to the Regent.

Mostly, however, Charles went his own way, seen constantly at White's with his cronies, gambling as heavily as ever, and drinking far more than was good for him. Bess paid the bills without comment, and he, despising himself because he was relying on her purse, grew colder towards her than ever.

Only once did Bess chide him, and to pay her out for her insolence he had an *affaire* with a Cyprian, who had had her eye on him for some time.

They met at a discreet house, and Charles did his best to fall in love with the girl, Madeline Knighton. It was not only that he wanted to hurt Bess: he wanted to drown what he felt about his own wife, which he didn't fully understand, in the white, rounded arms of the girl he now slept with.

He watched her brushing her long dark hair, sweeping the heavy locks over bare shoulders as creamy as fresh milk. She was a most delectable sight: full-breasted, with plump hips, and long, shapely legs. He couldn't conceive why she didn't arouse excitement in him, nor why, when she crossed to the bed, his loins didn't ache to possess her.

"Does your wife know about me?" Madeline slipped between the sheets, kissing the corner of his mouth. "Is she angry?"

"I don't know, and I don't care."

It was a lie, but Madeline chuckled with feline satisfaction.

"I expect she does. Plenty of kind friends to tell her about us, my sweet. And if she doesn't approve she can always take a lover herself, can't she?"

Barron's mouth thinned.

"Don't talk nonsense."

"It isn't nonsense. My dear, do you suppose that she won't pay you out in your own coin? Besides, she's considered a beauty, isn't she, although to my mind she's too thin, and I've never favoured hair that colour. What is more, she's a sight too haughty."

Charles, in his vexation, almost laughed. Bess, haughty? The common chit he had almost rundown one night, which seemed a lifetime ago, and whose dirty face and luscious body had filled him with an instant and undying desire.

"Don't talk about my wife." He lay back in the candlelight, watching Madeline. "She has nothing to do with you and me."

Madeline sniggered again.

"Jealous? How very provincial, sweet. Why, no one is jealous of his own wife nowadays, and I do hear that Lord Carleton has quite set his heart on capturing Lady Barron."

"She wouldn't give him a second look."

"My informants say differently." The girl leaned over Barron, letting him feel the warmth of her nakedness against him. "Some say that she is very taken with him, and is often seen riding with him."

"Will you shut up!" Barron was violent as he grabbed Madeline's hair and made her squeal. "I haven't come here to listen to some drab tittle-tattling."

"Drab!" Madeline tried to free herself, lips pinched. "I'm no drab, and you were glad enough to take me when you wanted me."

The irritation in Charles drained away. What was the use? The wretched woman was right. There were strong hints about Bess and Stephen Carleton, but Charles had shut his ears to them.

"Very well, you're not a drab, and I do want you."

"That's better." She was all sweet compliance again. "Then shew me, dearest, just how much you need me."

He knew that he should have left things alone, but the next morning, when he and Bess had left their separate bedrooms and descended to take breakfast together, he said curtly:

"There is talk about you and Carleton. I don't like it."

Bess kept her smile to herself.

"Really?"

"Yes, really!" Her indifference infuriated him. "I won't have you behaving like a doxy, even if you are one."

"A doxy." She was faintly amused, and now she let him see it. "Like Madeline Knighton, you mean?"

He was a little whiter round the mouth.

"That is an entirely different matter."

"Do you think so?" Still unruffled, she sipped her hot chocolate and gazed at him innocently over the rim of the cup. "It seems remarkably similar to me."

"Then you are blind," he said roughly. "A man may . . . well . . . a man can . . . "

" . . . romp in any harlot's bed, but Charles Barron's wife must lead the life of a nun, is that it? My dear, you have chosen the wrong woman. You are in no position to dictate to me."

He swore aloud.

"Because I take your money, eh? I wondered how long it would be before you reminded me of that."

"I didn't mean any such thing," she said quickly. "I meant that if you can take a woman whenever you fancy, there is no reason why . . . "

"Damn you to hell," shouted Charles, and strode out of the room, leaving Bess fighting for self-control.

It wasn't working out as she had hoped it would. Charles had demanded his own room, and never once came to hers. He ignored her, as if she were part of the furniture, and took even less interest in his son.

She found Stephen Carleton rather a bore, but he was an eager suitor, and she wasn't going to let Charles think her a door-mat for him to tread on. She wondered whether his furious exit had been born of jealousy, or wounded pride, and decided, reluctantly, that it was the latter. He didn't want her; he had made that painfully obvious. It was simply that he thought he would look a cuckold in his friends' eyes if she and Stephen became the object of too much talk.

Brummell regarded the relationship between Charles and Bess with weary amusement. He glanced at Barron in the mirror as he began to arrange the third stock of the morning.

"Sour, Charles?"

"No."

The bleak response made the small, pouting lips move slightly. Really, Charles was so obtuse it was hardly credible.

"Too much wine last night, or is the fair Cyprian tiring you?"

"Neither." Barron glared at the Beau.

"Can one not be silent for two minutes without being thought farouche?"

"Indeed one can." Brummell put his head on one side and debated the question of whether the left fold was too narrow. "Yes, m'dear fellow, naturally one can, but not for as long as your silences last."

He laughed aloud as Barron got up and shut the door hard behind him.

"You know, Robinson," he said, untying the stock and handing it to his valet. "A rake, yes; a heedless gambler, yes; a madman when he rides those curricles of his at such a pace, yes." He took the fourth stock and began again. "But never did I think to live to say that Charles Barron was a fool." He nodded. "Yes, that's better. Now the gloves, if you please. I must be on my way to White's and make my peace with Sir Charles, although God knows he doesn't deserve such a favour. A cretin, Robinson, that's what he is; a cretin."

"Yes, sir." Robinson opened the door, and the immaculate Mr Brummell sauntered out to let the world have its first peep of that day's sartorial triumph.

* * *

The blank, loveless existence of Charles and Bess continued. Often she lay awake at night, knowing he was only a few yards away, longing for him with such intensity that the pain was almost unbearable.

He never touched her. A brief bow was all that she ever got from him, and when she was alone she raged aloud that some pert miss was getting the kisses and satisfaction which she, Bess, yearned for.

She took particular care over her toilet, always appearing with every hair in place, each gown more fashionable than the last, but it made no difference. Charles hardly looked at her, and she might as well have been in the rags she had worn when they had first met.

But Charles did notice, although he never let Bess see it. He watched her grace and proud carriage; the glint on her red-gold hair; the sheen of her skin, and the rose-red seduction of her mouth.

They kept their thoughts to themselves until one night when Barron returned in the early hours, rather the worse for drink. Bess was still up, wandering along the corridor because she couldn't sleep, tormented by the certainty that Charles was with that hateful cat Madeline Knighton.

When he saw her, candle-stick in hand, he paused. The shift was nearly transparent, and it sobered him as if someone had thrown a bucket of water over him.

"Why are you still up?" he asked curtly. "Spying on me?"

She was very close to him, and he could smell the musky perfume she used. It made him feel giddy, as did the outline of her small, perfect breasts.

"No." For once she didn't spit back. "I couldn't sleep. I thought you were already abed."

She was willing him to stretch out his hand to her; praying that he would bend his head and touch her lips with his own.

"I see."

He was beginning to feel a surge of desire which he knew he wouldn't be able to control, taking the candle from her and placing it on a table outside his bedroom.

She closed her eyes, standing very still and passive, letting him make the first move, holding her breath as his fingers moved up her arms, allowing herself to lean slightly towards him.

She remained quiet as he drew the shift down to her waist, not daring to look at him. She let him take her hand, leading her into his room, and only then did she speak.

"Charles . . . I . . . "

Her lips parted and she opened her eyes to share the precious moment with him. It was so close: his hold on her was tightening, and the passion she had held in check for so long was rising like a flood-tide.

Then she found herself thrust away, gasping at the expression on his face.

"You are just like Augusta," he said in a soft, deadly whisper. "You bought me, as she wanted to do, not just because you wished to shame and disgrace me, as you promised you would do, but to be your plaything whenever you wanted to satisfy your lust. Well, Bess Hathaway, you won't do it with me. I don't need you: I don't want you! Get out! Get out of my room, and stay out; you sicken me!"

She fled, pulling the shift up as she ran. In the seclusion of her own bedroom she no longer tried to hide the terrible grief which racked her body. It was no use; he didn't want her. He would never want her now, and things couldn't go on as they were.

She couldn't live with him another day, loving him as she did, knowing how he felt about her. Whatever the future held, it couldn't be a worse torture than this. To-morrow she would make the necessary arrangements. That night she gave over to tears.

Charles lay on his bed, eyes closed. She was a scheming bitch to lure him so, when all she wanted was revenge. Bad enough that she had to keep him; worse that she made a mockery of what he felt for her. He couldn't get the sight of her body out of his mind. The perfume still lingered in the air, and he clenched his fingers tightly by his side to stop himself going to her and taking her there and then.

It couldn't go on. Whatever else

happened, it wouldn't be as bad as the destruction he and Bess were inflicting on each other. He would have to leave, for the next time she came to him like that, for whatever reason, he knew he wouldn't have the strength to resist.

In the morning he would tell Bess that he was going. The rest of the night was given over to deep sorrow which he couldn't control. Bess had succeeded; her promise had been made good. She had made his heart grovel, and for that, he assured himself grimly, he would never forgive her.

* * *

Charles left for Brighton as soon as it was light, his curricle hurtling along the road at breakneck speed.

Bess, very composed, with not a tear to be seen, sat with Christine and told her of her plans.

"You are leaving?" Christine was aghast. "But the baby . . . "

"He will stay with you." The seering pain of having to leave her child was concealed as carefully as the rest of her emotions. "You will look after him, and he will be under his father's protection. Don't worry. He will do well enough."

"But why must you go, and surely there is no need for you to return to that kind of life?"

Miss Cotter's nose twitched. Bess had made her announcement baldly, and without compromise. All her worldly possessions, save the few things she was to take with her, were to be put at the disposal of Sir Charles. Her clothes and jewels, she said, could be sold, even the house, if necessary. She would take sufficient money to pay for lodgings in Kensington, and enough to buy a modest brothel in that district.

"But why?"

Bess gave a small, tight smile at Christine's anguish.

"Why not? It's a way of earning a living."

"But you don't need to work."

"I do." She was drawing the rings off her fingers. "I need to work until I drop. That way I don't have to think. Besides, I started as a brothel-keeper, and that's how I'll finish. That's all Charles sees in me, and perhaps he's right. I flew too high: now it's time I became myself again. He hates to take money from me, I know. Now all of it will be his, and he won't have to hate me for that, at least."

Christine put out a tentative hand, half-afraid of being rejected.

"Have you ever told him how you feel about him?"

Bess sat up straighter.

"How I feel about him?"

"Yes, if he knew . . . "

"He already knows that I think him a wastrel and a boor."

The seamstress sniffed, fishing for her handkerchief.

"Yes, you've told him that, I've no doubt, but what of the rest? The thing which really matters."

The eyes of the two women met. Then Bess said slowly:

"I'll never tell him that. Never give him the opportunity of laughing in my face. He'll always think of me as a low-born harlot, and he'll have nothing to do with me for the rest of his life because I paid him out for what he did to me. He says

I bought him, and I suppose I did, in a way, but not for the reason he thinks."

"Then tell him the truth, before it is too late."

"It's already too late." Bess rose and patted Christine's hand. "Don't upset yourself, love. It wasn't meant to be, and that's that. You'll always be cared for; I've seen to that. I've left a letter for Charles about you and the boy, and whatever else he does, he won't ignore that."

In the dark old house in a shabby corner of Kensington, Bess threw herself completely into her new life. No luxury this time, for she had brought with her only enough money to make a start: the house would have to pay for itself. She went down on her hands and knees with the two scrubbing women she had taken on, glad to be utterly exhausted when the night came, so that she slept as soon as her head touched the pillow.

During the day she hadn't time to think either. There were curtains to make and sheets to stitch; floors to cover; suitable girls to be found. It came easily to Bess, because she had done it all before, and once the initial labour was over the place began to flourish.

The men who came to the house were often more interested in Bess than they were in the girls, but she gave them all short shrift.

"Not me," she would say with a bright, impersonal smile. "Upstairs to the left; you'll like her. I've got other things to do."

She longed for news of her child, and of Charles, but she had warned Christine not to write, in case Barron heard of it. Since Roger Burnham could no longer be relied upon, the only tidings which reached her were the odd scraps of gossip from her clients.

She kept well away from the centre of London, for there she would have been recognised, and even her maids commented that it was odd that Mrs Charles never seemed to go out in the daytime.

In the early hours of the morning, when the house was quiet, and business was over, she would slip out into the foggy air, moving quickly and noiselessly over the cobbles until she found herself thinking. Then she would rush back and begin some pointless piece of housework until dawn came, and the bustle of the day was in full swing once more.

She began to make rather a lot of money. It really was ironic that she seemed to attract money like bees to a honeypot, when Charles could do nothing but lose it. She wondered if he were gambling as heavily, and whether he was still making love to the Knighton woman.

To punish herself for allowing her thoughts to stray to such things, she worked harder than ever, sleeping less, eating less, until her slimness became something more worrying, but she didn't care. Charles wasn't there to see how her clothes hung on her, and the way her eyes were smudged with fatigue, and no one else mattered.

She thought she was doing rather well, until one night two young bucks came adventuring in shabby Mallerby Street where Bess's establishment was situated.

They had dined rather too extravagantly, and the wine had gone to their heads, yet their talk, although loose, was easy enough to comprehend.

"Beau Barron's back from Brighton," said one, and gave a snort of laughter. "Looks like the devil too. Bumped into him myself at Waiters's; thought he was goin' to fell me to the ground. Ah, madam, my thanks."

Bess put a glass of wine in front of the men. It was her custom to provide a measure of refreshment before she took their money, and guided them to the upper regions of the house.

"Know the Beau, do you, m'm?" asked the other, a plump youth with a gaudy waistcoat straining across his stomach. "Ladies love him, so they say, but I'd not like to cross him."

"No." Bess was seething with excitement, praying the two men would go on, but keeping all sign of her longing from her face. "I don't think I've ever heard of him."

They shouted with mirth.

"Not heard of Mad Barron, m'm? Why, where have you been? All London talks of him, and his women. Rides like a fiend, and chances higher stakes than anyone I know."

"He sounds . . . imprudent, sir. However, I'm sure he wouldn't come here. Not fashionable enough, is it?"

"Don't know." The taller man was eyeing her thoughtfully. Too thin, but one could have drowned in those eyes. "Does for us. Must mention it to the Beau."

"I don't think that would be a good idea." Bess felt fear tighten her stomach-muscles and make the palms of her hands sweat. "I like to run a quiet place, you see. This . . . man might make trouble for me."

"Daresay I could be persuaded to hold my tongue." The buck rose, taking her hand. "Denby Harland, at your service. Now, suppose we go upstairs and discuss the matter."

Bess was in a panic.

"What matter? There's nothing to discuss."

"Oh, but there is." His moist hand was fondling her arm intimately. "Could easily steer Sir Charles this way, you know."

She had enough wit to say:

"Sir Charles? Who is he?"

"The Beau, of course. Ah, but then you don't know him, do you? Well, what d'yer say? Shall you become acquainted with him, or shall we adjourn?"

Numb, Bess led the way up to her room. She wanted no part of the obnoxious fop, but she dared not risk Charles finding out where she was, no matter what the cost.

Harland looked round the room approvingly.

"Yes, very nice. Good taste for a bro . . . "

"A brothel-keeper?"

"Well . . . yes."

He looked at her more carefully, conscious of the change in her tone.

"Some of us learn quickly," said Bess after a second, for she didn't want to answer any more questions. "But I think you would be better served in the next room."

"Doubt that." Denby grinned. "Not much flesh on you, but I don't mind that. Come on now, don't be stand-offish. Give me a kiss, there's a good girl."

Bess never understood what made her break down then. She had gone through so much, keeping her self-control holding her head high, but as Harland caught her wrist, she started to cry. Not gentle tears to move him, but deep, shuddering gulps which shook her to pieces.

Harland was horrified, for he was not an unkind man. The sight of Bess drove the last of the brandy from his mind, and he said quickly:

"M'm! I say, m'm . . . don't . . . don't do that. Didn't think it meant so much to you. Wouldn't have pushed myself, if I'd thought . . . "

Bess went on crying, and Denby drew her to a chair and got her to sit down, patting her shoulder helplessly.

"Shall I call someone," he asked finally, looking longingly at the door. This wasn't at all what he had bargained for, and the woman whom he had desired not five minutes before was now a lodestone round his neck. "I'll get . . . someone . . . "

"No, no!" Bess shook her head, gasping as the worst of the sobs died down. "No, please don't tell anyone. Will you leave me? I'm sorry . . . I . . . it isn't you. It's not you who . . . "

"No, quite. Just so. Well, I'll be going then."

Downstairs, he met his companion, and hurried him away.

"An armful was she?" asked his friend as they got into their carriage. "Too much like a stick for my taste."

Denby Harland was young and thoughtless, but he was a gentleman, and he was also ashamed of himself.

"Good enough," he said, and dismissed the subject before any more could be said. "Well, that's that. Let's go back to the Coterie Club."

He gave the darkened house one more glance. The oddest to-do: he'd never known anything like it before, but it had taught him a lesson he would never forget.

The depths of human suffering were limitless, and he knew it would be a very long time before he forgot the look of stark despair in the eyes of Mrs Charles.

* * *

Christine Cotter held out against Barron for as long as she could. He tried every means of tricking her into an admission of knowing where Bess had gone; had threatened her with physical violence; had stormed round the house like one possessed.

When everything else had failed, he used the one trump-card which Christine could not withstand.

"I'll send the boy to the workhouse."

Christine moaned.

"You couldn't! Sir Charles, you wouldn't! He's your own son."

He was implaccable.

"I can and I will. Now, where is she?"

"I promised . . . "

"To hell with your promises. Get the child."

"No!"

"Then tell me where she is."

He listened grimly.

"A whore-house, eh? Yes, she's reverted to type I see. Well, so be it."

"She won't want to see you."

"Mind your own business."

"I didn't mean to interfere, but . . . "

"Then keep quiet!" He looked so fearsome that Christine drew back. "Look after my son, and tend to your sewing, but keep your nose out of my business, you old . . . "

At No 10 Mallerby Street he drew his horses to a halt. It was bitterly cold that January, ice and snow laying traps for the unwary. There was a couple saying good-night in the doorway of No 10. He pushed past them without ceremony, and shouted to the abigail who was about to mount the stairs.

"Here, you! Yes, you, my girl. Where's your mistress? Where's the keeper of this cat-house?"

Bess heard him, and almost fainted. Even the anger in his voice did not stop it from being the sweetest sound she had ever heard, yet it took much courage to open the door of her sitting-room and emerge to face him.

Charles swung round, and stopped dead. Bess looked terrible. All the lovely colour had gone from her cheeks, and she was so thin that he scarcely recognised her.

"We can't talk here," he said finally, conscious of the maid's stare, and two roistering drunks stumbling downstairs.

"Is this your room?"

Without waiting for a reply he steered her through the door, turning her to face him.

"In God's name, what's wrong with you? Are you ill? And why here, in this benighted place? Are you bereft of your senses?"

"No, I'm not ill." She felt weak at his touch, holding on to his coat-sleeve to prevent herself from falling. "Just tired."

"Why?" He got her to a chair, standing over her. "In the name of pity, why? What are you doing here?"

"Running a brothel, just like I did before." She tried to smile, but the effort was too great. "Isn't that what you'd expect of me? You always said I was a bawd."

"Why did you go?"

"I couldn't live with you any longer."

"I see."

She wanted to cry out to him not to look like that: to say that he had misunderstood, but she couldn't.

"You had no need to go. If my presence was so repugnant to you I would have left. In any event, you're coming back with me."

"No!"

"Yes! I'll drag you out of the house by your hair if I have to."

"No, oh, have some pity, Charles. Leave me be."

"You're coming home."

"I'm not! I'm not! You can't make me . . . ah!"

She gasped aloud as he jerked her to her feet.

"I can make you, have no fear of that."

Their bodies were touching, each sensing something very strong and powerful, but both refusing to acknowledge it.

"I . . . can't. I don't want to live with you, Charles, ever again."

The silence went on for a long time. His hands were on her shoulders, and she could feel the beat of her heart against his chest. He was on the point of blurting out what he was thinking, when she whispered again:

"I won't come back to you. I cannot bear you near me."

He let her go, as if his fingers had

been burned, the mask dropping down to conceal his expression.

"Very well. I had not realised just how repellent you found me. My apologies, madam; I shall not bother you again."

"Thank you."

Her lips were so stiff that she could hardly get the words out, conscious that he was walking out of her life for the last time.

"One thing."

"Yes?" She dared not look at him. "What is it?"

"See a physician. I don't want your death on my conscience."

"I'm all right."

"Do as I say." He rapped the words out. "Hate me, if you will, but don't kill yourself in the doing. I'm not worth it, Bess. You should know that by now."

The door closed behind him, and Bess sat down again. It wasn't likely that he would come back, not after what he thought she had meant.

"Oh, lovey," she whispered unhappily. "You didn't understand. Dearest Charles, why do you never understand?"

9

CHARLES played the final card, and a roar of approval and excitement ran round Boodle's.

Barron's run of bad luck was well and truly over, and in the past three weeks he had won thousands of pounds. Now, in his latest flirtation with Fortune, he had acquired the manor and green rolling acres of Cranton, set in the idyllic valley of the Wye.

James Whyster, the former master of Cranton, shrugged indifferently. He'd never liked the place; too far from town and his friends. He'd called it his country mausoleum, and Barron was welcome to it.

"Well done, Charles." Brummell, poised and unruffled as ever, raised his wine-glass to him. "I swear you're becoming a veritable Midas these days. Everything you touch turns to gold, yet you don't look in the least pleased about it. Don't you like Cranton?"

"I've never seen it." Barron didn't smile. He wasn't thinking about Whyster's lost inheritance, but about Bess, and the way she had looked when he had last seen her. Seen her, and heard her say that she couldn't bear to be near to him. "Doubt if I ever will."

"Seems a pity." The Beau's gaze was travelling round the room, ignoring eager eyes which sought his nod. "Told it's a handsome place."

Barron didn't reply, and Brummell sighed.

"M'dear fellow, never one to interest myself in other men's private affairs, as I've said before. Far too exhausting, and no one's ever grateful for one's efforts. Besides, it takes my mind off the important things of life."

"Like the cut of your coat?"

"Precisely." The Beau was unmoved by Charles's acerbic rejoinder. "But in your case, I propose to make an exception."

"Do you, by God!" Charles gave Brummell a hard look. "Be advised, George, don't meddle in my business, or you'll regret it."

"Probably will, but there's no help

for it. Can't put up with you as you are now for another day. You're as sullen as a spurned apple-wife. You don't ride any more; don't eat; only come to the tables twice a week, although I'm bound to admit that even these limited excursions have been remarkably successful. But you don't enjoy what you're doing. Damn it, Charles, I'm told you don't even look at women nowadays."

"So?"

Barron's temper was rising.

"So, it's time someone told you the truth about yourself."

"If there's anyone bold enough to risk a thrashing for it."

"For heaven's sake!" The Beau gave Charles an exasperated glance. "Do stop behaving like a schoolboy, and pay attention to what I'm saying. You're a fool."

"Thank you!"

"Don't interrupt. You're a fool, as I say, because you're in love with your own wife, and don't even realise it. Very bad taste, of course, and quite hopelessly unfashionable, but that's the measure of it. I see no help for it; you'll have to tell her."

"Never!" Charles was quietly violent. "I'll never do that. She has made it plain enough how she feels about me. She said she couldn't bear me near her. What's simpler than that?"

Brummell took a pinch of snuff, making a small ceremony out of the easy turn of his wrist, drawing fresh, admiring glances from those watching.

"Do you know, I sometimes wonder if you are not mentally defective. Can't you see what Elizabeth was saying to you? Don't you know anything about women, after all these years of sharing their beds?"

"I've no idea what you're talking about."

Barron's nostrils were pinched, his mouth like a trap.

"Then you'd better go and ask Elizabeth to explain it to you. And please do it soon, for we're all getting profoundly tired of your long face."

"I haven't the faintest notion what Brummell was trying to say," said Charles later to Pengelly, whilst the latter was easing off the velvet evening-coat. "What business is it of his, anyway?"

"None, sir, of course, but your friends don't like to see you this way." Pengelly smoothed the material with loving fingers. "Neither do I, if I may make so bold."

"Not you too! Confound it, man, don't you understand? She doesn't want me."

"Now my experience of the fair sex," went on the valet as if Barron hadn't spoken, "is that whatever they say, they mean the opposite. Very confusing, until one gets the measure of it; then it's no problem. Found it so with my Meg. Led me a real dance, the little minx, till I saw what was what. Then I had no more trouble."

"My wife won't receive me." It was an admission Charles would have made to few men, but Pengelly was a true and trusted servant. "Can't even get near her."

The valet chuckled.

"Then someone else must get to her."

Charles frowned.

"You mean an emissary to plead my case? No, I won't . . . "

"An emissary, if you like, and what

better one could you choose than your son?"

Barron's hand was stilled on his snuff-box.

"My son? What the devil do you mean? Are you suggesting I should send an infant into that whore-house? I'd die, before I saw him there."

"So would his mother," returned Pengelly slyly. "That'ud bring her to her senses, and then she'd have to talk to you."

Barron didn't move for a full two minutes; then he began to smile.

"Pengelly, you're a rogue, but a wily one. Here, buy your Meg a trifle with this."

He threw a handful of gold coins on the table, and started to laugh.

"Yes, by all that's holy, you're right. She'd have to talk to me then, wouldn't she?"

* * *

It was with delight that Bess received the news that Christine Cotter was waiting for her in the hall of No 10 Mallerby

Street. She was desperately anxious for news of her baby, and hurried down the stairs, stopping short when she saw the unhappiness on Christine's face, and the child wrapped in a shawl in her arms.

"Christine! Are you mad? Why have you brought Charlie here? I trusted you . . ."

Miss Cotter was distraught.

"I know, I know! I pleaded with Sir Charles not to make me bring the boy to a place like this, but he wouldn't listen. I even went down on my knees to him, but he only laughed at me. Oh, Lady Barron, he laughed at me."

"Don't . . . Christine, don't! Here, come into my sitting-room. We don't want the whole world to hear us."

She herded the pair of them into her sanctum, settling Christine in an armchair, and taking the baby in her arms. He smiled at her, and she could feel a swift pang. He was so like his father, that simply to look at him was painful.

"Did he say anything? Give you a note for me?"

"Not a note." Miss Cotter blew her

nose, and tried to regain her composure. "But he said he didn't want the child with him any longer, and that you would have to take him."

"But I can't have him here! Charles must see that."

"He said that it was your choice to come to a place like this. If you want to condemn your own son to life in a brothel, that is your business. Oh, that's not what I feel, dear lady Barron, but what Sir Charles told me to say."

"I can believe it." Bess was bitter. "He's a heartless, unfeeling monster, but he won't score over me this way. I shall take the boy back to his rightful home, and my husband will have to keep him there. God knows I paid a high enough price to ensure that."

"No, my dear Bess," said Charles blandly, when Bess held out her child. "I'm having none of him, not without you. Can't think why you left here. Comfortable enough place, ain't it? An improvement on that hell-hole in Mallerby Street."

Her eyes were very green, a sure sign that an explosion was not far off.

"Oh yes, it's comfortable enough, and that's why the child is going to stay here."

"No, he's not."

Bess glared at Barron who was lounging easily against the carved mantelpiece, making no attempt to take the baby from her. He looked as bored as ever, but she thought that awful, haunted look had left him, and even in the depths of her rage she could see a change in him. A kind of smug satisfaction. It fed her own temper, and she shouted at him.

"Damn you to Hades, Charles Barron! Haven't you a spark of decency left in you? This is your own son. Do you really want him brought up in a brothel?"

"No, I want him brought up here, but with you."

"I've told you; I'm not coming back."

"Then neither is your son."

"God, how I hate you!"

"So you have said, many times, in many ways."

Bess saw none of the anger in him which she had encountered at their last meeting. Indeed, he seemed almost amused at her outburst. She tried another way, forcing herself not to lay the boy down and claw Charles's face with her finger-nails.

"Please." It was hard to beg, but she made herself do it. "I implore you. Don't make our child suffer because of me. It is so unfair."

"Life is unfair, hadn't you noticed?"

He was still indifferent, but she thought the corners of his mouth turned up slightly, as if a laugh wasn't far away.

"I . . . I . . . can't come back, you know that."

"It's your decision." He let the heavy-lidded eyes move slowly over her, as if he were stripping her of her gown and what she wore beneath it. "Entirely up to you."

She knew she was blushing, not with anger this time, but because of the way Charles was looking at her, and what that look was doing to her.

"I'll . . . I'll . . . have to think about it."

"Do so, by all means, and let me know your decision. Meanwhile, take the boy with you. He's not staying here."

Back at Mallerby Street she burst into tears.

"Oh, Christine, he's so hard. It was like talking to a marble statue. He dislikes me so much, he's even willing to ruin his son's life to pay me out. He won't take my little love, at least, not without me."

Christine had been full of concern, her own eyes wet, but sudddenly she dabbed the drops away and considered Bess's bent head. She hadn't known any men herself, and so her experience was limited to what she had seen going on around her, but even her vicarious experience was enough to make her pause.

She had accepted unquestioningly that the wicked Sir Charles was punishing his wife, and was capable of stooping to the most appalling depths to hurt her. Yet, if he really detested Bess as much as that, why did he want her back? Simply to look after a baby which any competent abigail could do just as well?

Miss Cotter stroked Bess's hair, and smiled to herself. Even she knew that lovers were not always rational. Sir Charles and Lady Elizabeth were no exception. She would have to think over the problem that night and see what she, Christine Cotter, could do to give the foolish pair a gentle shove.

* * *

That evening, before Miss Cotter had a chance to plot, Sir David Romney called at No 10 Mallerby Street. He, and the friends he had brought with him, had drunk a great deal, swaying and lurching as they piled into the narrow hall, and demanded more wine, and then some women.

When Romney came face to face with Bess, he stopped, and she could feel the colour draining from her cheeks, for they had met several times before in polite drawing-rooms and on the floor at Almack's ball.

"Know you, don't I?" asked Sir David, belching loudly. "Never forget a face. Where've we met before?"

"We haven't, sir." Bess was rigid with fear. "I would have remembered."

"Yes, yes we have." He was insistent. "I tell you, I can always recollect a face."

"I have only just arrived here from Liverpool." Bess hoped the lie sounded more convincing to him than it did to her. "Just a day or two ago."

Romney stared a moment longer, but then a girl with long blonde hair and a skimpy shift came down the stairs to claim his attention, and he turned away from Bess.

"I'll have to leave here, Christine," she said, when all the men had left the house. "You can see how risky it would be for me to stay."

"But where will you go?" Christine was worried. She hadn't had time to lay her plans. "Where will you take the boy?"

"I shan't take Charlie with me." Bess sat upright, hands clenched in her lap. "I shall go to America. I know of others who have gone there."

"Not people of your class."

Bess managed a shaky laugh.

"You forget what my class really is. I'm Bess of the stews, remember? Yes, I shall go with all the other poor people who are trying to make a new life for themselves."

"It will be so hard."

"Probably, but I'm used to that."

"You've no money. You left it all for Sir Charles, and, from what I hear, he doesn't need it any more. He's been so lucky lately, I'm told, that he is getting to be one of the richest men in London. Why don't you ask him to return your money?"

"I shan't ask him for anything," Bess replied shortly. "I shan't even see him again. I'll give you a letter for him. Take it to him, with my sweet Charlie. He won't be able to return him this time, for I shall be gone. As to money, I've made enough from this place to keep me for quite a while."

"There must be another way! Oh, Lady Barron, please reconsider what you are doing. It is so final."

"I have considered it." Bess rose and went to her writing-table. "There isn't an alternative. If I stay in England my husband will not accept his son. The boy must be with him; it's only right. I can't give my son what Charles can."

Charles Barron read Bess's letter, turning away from Christine in case some hint of his feelings should become apparent to her.

'Don't look for me, I beg you,' Bess had written. 'I can never come back to you, but not for the reason you think. I can't return because I love you so much, and to try to live with you, knowing how contemptuous you are of me, is too hard to bear. I'm not brave enough. I worship you, dearest Charles, with all my heart, but you'll never forget what I was. In spite of my finery, and how Christine and Roger taught me to speak, it didn't hide it from you, did it? All you ever saw was Bess the whore.'

Charles folded the letter very carefully and put it in his pocket before he turned back to Miss Cotter.

"Do you know what is in this note?"

She coughed discreetly.

"Not exactly, of course, Sir Charles. Just that Lady Barron is going away, and has returned the boy to your care. I left him with a maid."

"Yes," Charles was looking at her thoughtfully, "but you know where my wife has gone, don't you? She would have told you."

"I was sworn to secrecy."

"No doubt, but I want to know, and

I'll stop at nothing to make you tell me. Do you understand me, Miss Cotter?"

He looked so frightening that Christine shrank back in her chair.

"Yes . . . yes, I understand."

"Then will you tell me readily, or do I have to use force?"

Miss Cotter's moment of nervousness was gone, and she gave a small laugh.

His face was like thunder.

"You find this amusing? I can assure you it isn't, as you will soon find out."

"Yes, I confess it has a laughable side, Sir Charles." Miss Cotter adjusted a fold in her skirt, head on one side. "And you had no need to threaten me, for I had every intention of telling you where my dearest Elizabeth had gone. I love her, you see."

Their eyes met. At first, there was no rapport, but then Charles sighed, and their silent communication was absolute.

Finally, he gave a crooked smile.

"You think I'm a fool too, don't you? Brummell does. He said so."

"All men in love are foolish, so I'm told. I think you ought to hurry. Lady Barron intends to sail to America, and is at this moment on her way to the docks. The ship is *The Heron*, and it is due to leave to-morrow morning. You'll find that she has taken a room at an inn called *The Cutlass*. I'm sure she shouldn't be there, for I suspect it is the most dangerous of places. I tried to make her change her mind, but she wouldn't listen."

"That doesn't surprise me," he said dryly, "but she'll listen to me, this time. Stay here, and wait for us. Look after our son."

"Gladly."

He touched Miss Cotter's shoulder.

"You have a great deal of patience. Most women would have walked out on the pair of us long ago."

Christine was very pink.

"Patience and love are closely connected, sir."

"Not between Bess and me, but never mind."

He left Miss Cotter gasping at his kiss he had planted on her cheek, and shouted to the grooms to get his curricle ready.

"Fastest horses!" he barked. "No time to waste."

In a matter of minutes he was gone, leaving his servants scratching their heads in perplexity, and Miss Cotter peeping through the window, smiling gently, and offering up a prayer that the mad Sir Charles would not break his neck before he reached the harbour.

* * *

Bess looked round the noisy, smelly parlour of *The Cutlass*, her heart sinking. There were two dozen or more packed into the confined space, all shabby and desperate to get away from England to the new world which might offer them more chance of survival.

It would take a long time to reach their destination, and some would die on the voyage, but they didn't care. They talked and laughed and swore, drinking cheap beer, and assuaging their hunger with great hunks of bread and cheese.

The Heron was a small vessel, and would take the party only as far as Liverpool. After that they would embark upon *The King's Trooper* which would carry them across the fierce Atlantic, to an alien land which had just shaken off the yoke of British rule and would not be at all pleased to welcome refugees from her late master's domain.

She went up to her bedroom, no larger than a cupboard, which had nothing to offer except a truckle bed, none too clean, a chair, and a table which rocked at the slightest touch.

She had schooled herself not to think. To think of Charles, the baby, and all those whom she was leaving behind would have been to weaken her resolve so devastatingly that she would have run back to London, and to the insoluble problem of loving a man who had no time for her.

She turned as she heard the tap on the door, fearful in case it was one of the rough-necks from below seeking a way of passing a dull evening.

The sight of Charles took every atom of colour from her face, and in spite of herself she took an involuntary step towards him.

He didn't say anything, forcing the first words out of her.

"What . . . what are you doing here?

How did you know where I was? Surely Christine didn't . . . she wouldn't . . . unless you . . . "

"I forced her to tell me."

He thought she was the loveliest thing he had ever seen, in spite of the plain dress and the pallor of her cheeks. He wanted her so much, yet there was a barrier to cross, and it was a difficult one. There had been so much acrimony between them; so many quarrels.

"How could you!" She was near to tears. "Why do you punish me so? Have you come to gloat over me because of my stupid confession? Is that it?"

"Of course not." He frowned quickly. "Don't be childish."

"Then what do you want?"

The scowl faded, and he said inconsequentially:

"You know, you really should eat more."

"So should you. Charles, what do you want?"

"You, of course." It was really quite simple to say when it came to it, and he couldn't think why he had feared it so. "You, my love; that's what I want."

"I . . . I . . . you don't mean it."

"For heaven's sake! Do you suppose I would race down here, to a hovel like this, simply to lie to you?"

"I can't believe it." She dared not let herself do so; Charles was too good at inflicting injuries. "It's a trick. You want to get back at me again."

"Dear God! Do you think I've got nothing better to do with my time?"

The irritation went, and in its place was cold determination.

"Bess, you're not getting on that ship. If you won't come with me, I'll kill you. I'd rather see you dead than belong to another man."

"There isn't another man." She was stunned by what she saw in his eyes. "Charles, there's never been another man. Only you."

"Fred, and that pompous ass, Crayford?"

"You knew they meant nothing to me. Oh, I was fond of poor Fred, but not like that. You've always known that."

"You've never made it plain before." He was longing to kiss her, but the moment was not ripe. "All I know is that I want you more than anything on earth. Without you there is nothing worth living for. Don't you realise that?"

Still she held back, and so did he. The gulf between them had only been spanned by words, and it wasn't enough.

"Come home," he said quietly. "We can't stay here. We'll return to London, and talk about this."

She didn't argue any more. Still not able to accept what he was saying, she could no longer refuse to go with him, but the journey was silent, neither wanting to be first to break the tension which seemed to have sprung up, nor to risk more suffering.

They dined alone, formally, like strangers, but when the servants withdrew Charles said shortly:

"If you think I'm going to live like this you're very much mistaken. Go upstairs and get your clothes off, Elizabeth."

Her lips parted, feeling a wonderful excitement running through her because he was looking at her in a way he had never done before.

"Don't you mean Bess the Whore?"

"All right." He shrugged. "Bess the

Whore, if that's how you think of yourself."

"It's how you think of me. How you've always thought of me."

"Once, perhaps, but not now."

He crossed the room, and over the gulf which had stretched between them, letting his fingers move slowly upwards, tightening on her shoulders. It was wonderfully familiar and comforting, yet in another way he felt as if he were about to make love to her for the first time.

"Bess, not any more."

She found her eyes were full of tears as she put one hand on his broad chest.

"I can't bear to be hurt again."

"Yes you can." He was blunt, refusing to pretend, for the future had to be based on honesty. "We'll fight, my dear. Ours won't be a peaceful union. I'll curse you sometimes; probably beat you too. And you. You'll rant and rave at me, and make my life a merry hell, I know you. But I'll love you all the days of my life. Isn't that what matters? Oh, my dearest, dearest, Bess, isn't that what really counts?"

The tears were streaming down her

face now, but she was the happiest woman in the world.

"Yes, that's what counts. I still can't believe it though. I'm afraid that I shall wake up in a moment and find myself in that horrid inn again, and you won't be there."

"I'm here." His arms tightened as their lips drew closer. "You won't get rid of me by waking up."

The kiss kept them locked together for a long time, the doubts, the pain, the anger, all washed away as they held each other tightly.

Then Charles gave a faint laugh.

"Go upstairs, you hussy, but don't expect to sleep." He kissed her again, his hand very gentle on her cheek. "We've so much wasted time to make up, sweetheart."

"Yes, we have." Reluctantly she released him. "I'll go, but come to me soon. I've waited so long for you, Charles, I can't wait any more."

He nodded, and then the last pain in her vanished, and she gave him a saucy wink.

"Right yer are, sir. I'll git me things

off, but when you comes, don't forgit yer five shillings."

He watched the door close behind her, his whole being soothed by the feel of her body against his, the touch of her mouth, and the unmistakable hunger he sensed in her. He wanted to shout and sing, to shew his happiness, but there wasn't time. Bess was waiting for him.

As he crossed the room he began to laugh.

"Five shillings, indeed," he said aloud. "You're getting above yourself, Bess my girl. You only cost me sixpence the first time, and sixpence is all you'll get to-night."

THE END

Other titles in the Ulverscroft Large Print Series:

TO FIGHT THE WILD
Rod Ansell and Rachel Percy

Lost in uncharted Australian bush, Rod Ansell survived by hunting and trapping wild animals, improvising shelter and using all the bushman's skills he knew.

COROMANDEL
Pat Barr

India in the 1830s is a hot, uncomfortable place, where the East India Company still rules. Amelia and her new husband find themselves caught up in the animosities which seethe between the old order and the new.

THE SMALL PARTY
Lillian Beckwith

A frightening journey to safety begins for Ruth and her small party as their island is caught up in the dangers of armed insurrection.

THE WILDERNESS WALK
Sheila Bishop

Stifling unpleasant memories of a misbegotten romance in Cleave with Lord Francis Aubrey, Lavinia goes on holiday there with her sister. The two women are thrust into a romantic intrigue involving none other than Lord Francis.

THE RELUCTANT GUEST
Rosalind Brett

Ann Calvert went to spend a month on a South African farm with Theo Borland and his sister. They both proved to be different from her first idea of them, and there was Storr Peterson — the most disturbing man she had ever met.

ONE ENCHANTED SUMMER
Anne Tedlock Brooks

A tale of mystery and romance and a girl who found both during one enchanted summer.

CLOUD OVER MALVERTON
Nancy Buckingham

Dulcie soon realises that something is seriously wrong at Malverton, and when violence strikes she is horrified to find herself under suspicion of murder.

AFTER THOUGHTS
Max Bygraves

The Cockney entertainer tells stories of his East End childhood, of his RAF days, and his post-war showbusiness successes and friendships with fellow comedians.

MOONLIGHT AND MARCH ROSES
D. Y. Cameron

Lynn's search to trace a missing girl takes her to Spain, where she meets Clive Hendon. While untangling the situation, she untangles her emotions and decides on her own future.

NURSE ALICE IN LOVE
Theresa Charles

Accepting the post of nurse to little Fernie Sherrod, Alice Everton could not guess at the romance, suspense and danger which lay ahead at the Sherrod's isolated estate.

POIROT INVESTIGATES
Agatha Christie

Two things bind these eleven stories together — the brilliance and uncanny skill of the diminutive Belgian detective, and the stupidity of his Watson-like partner, Captain Hastings.

LET LOOSE THE TIGERS
Josephine Cox

Queenie promised to find the long-lost son of the frail, elderly murderess, Hannah Jason. But her enquiries threatened to unlock the cage where crucial secrets had long been held captive.

THE TWILIGHT MAN
Frank Gruber

Jim Rand lives alone in the California desert awaiting death. Into his hermit existence comes a teenage girl who blows both his past and his brief future wide open.

DOG IN THE DARK
Gerald Hammond

Jim Cunningham breeds and trains gun dogs, and his antagonism towards the devotees of show spaniels earns him many enemies. So when one of them is found murdered, the police are on his doorstep within hours.

THE RED KNIGHT
Geoffrey Moxon

When he finds himself a pawn on the chessboard of international espionage with his family in constant danger, Guy Trent becomes embroiled in moves and countermoves which may mean life or death for Western scientists.

TIGER TIGER
Frank Ryan

A young man involved in drugs is found murdered. This is the first event which will draw Detective Inspector Sandy Woodings into a whirlpool of murder and deceit.

CAROLINE MINUSCULE
Andrew Taylor

Caroline Minuscule, a medieval script, is the first clue to the whereabouts of a cache of diamonds. The search becomes a deadly kind of fairy story in which several murders have an other-worldly quality.

LONG CHAIN OF DEATH
Sarah Wolf

During the Second World War four American teenagers from the same town join the Army together. Forty-two years later, the son of one of the soldiers realises that someone is systematically wiping out the families of the four men.

THE LISTERDALE MYSTERY
Agatha Christie

Twelve short stories ranging from the light-hearted to the macabre, diverse mysteries ingeniously and plausibly contrived and convincingly unravelled.

TO BE LOVED
Lynne Collins

Andrew married the woman he had always loved despite the knowledge that Sarah married him for reasons of her own. So much heartache could have been avoided if only he had known how vital it was to be loved.

ACCUSED NURSE
Jane Converse

Paula found herself accused of a crime which could cost her her job, her nurse's reputation, and even the man she loved, unless the truth came to light.

BUTTERFLY MONTANE
Dorothy Cork

Parma had come to New Guinea to marry Alec Rivers, but she found him completely disinterested and that overbearing Pierce Adams getting entirely the wrong idea about her.

HONOURABLE FRIENDS
Janet Daley

Priscilla Burford is happily married when she meets Junior Environment Minister Alistair Thurston. Inevitably, sexual obsession and political necessity collide.

WANDERING MINSTRELS
Mary Delorme

Stella Wade's career as a concert pianist might have been ruined by the rudeness of a famous conductor, so it seemed to her agent and benefactor. Even Sir Nicholas fails to see the possibilities when John Tallis falls deeply in love with Stella.

MORNING IS BREAKING
Lesley Denny

The growing frenzy of war catapults Diane Clements into a clandestine marriage and separation with a German refugee.

LAST BUS TO WOODSTOCK
Colin Dexter

A girl's body is discovered huddled in the courtyard of a Woodstock pub, and Detective Chief Inspector Morse and Sergeant Lewis are hunting a rapist and a murderer.

THE STUBBORN TIDE
Anne Durham

Everyone advised Carol not to grieve so excessively over her cousin's death. She might have followed their advice if the man she loved thought that way about her, but another girl came first in his affections.